I0673056

THE PAGE TURNERS

BOOK ONE

STREET MAP OF

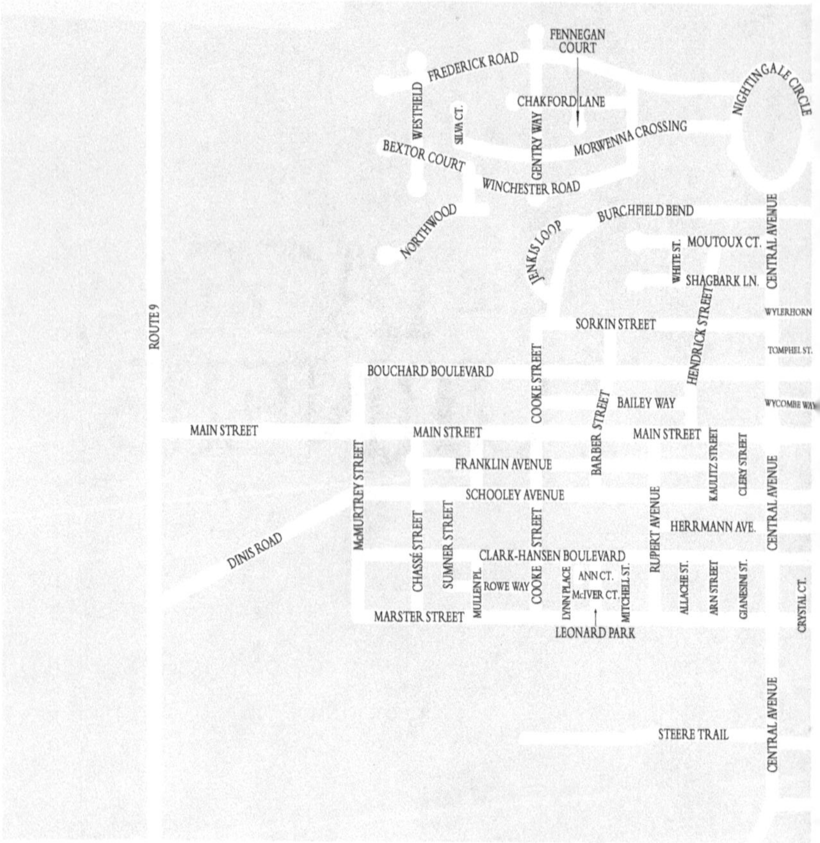

FENNEGAN COURT

FREDERICK ROAD

CHAKFORD LANE

WESTFIELD

SILVA CT.

GENTRY WAY

MORWENNA CROSSING

NIGHTINGALE CIRCLE

BEXTOR COURT

WINCHESTER ROAD

BURCHFIELD BEND

NORTHWOOD

JENKIS LOOP

WHITE ST.

MOUTOUX CT.

CENTRAL AVENUE

SHAGBARK LN.

HENDRICK STREET

WYLERHORN

SORKIN STREET

TOMPHEL ST.

COOKE STREET

BOUCHARD BOULEVARD

BAILEY WAY

WYCOMBE WAY

ROUTE 9

MAIN STREET

MAIN STREET

BARBER STREET

MAIN STREET

KALLITZ STREET

CLERY STREET

FRANKLIN AVENUE

McMURTREY STREET

SCHOOLEY AVENUE

RUPERT AVENUE

CENTRAL AVENUE

HERRMANN AVE.

DINIS ROAD

CHASSÉ STREET

SUMNER STREET

COOKE STREET

CLARK-HANSEN BOULEVARD

MULLEN PL.

ROWE WAY

ANN CT.

LYNN PLACE

McIVER CT.

MITCHELL ST.

ALLACHE ST.

ANN STREET

GIANSINNI ST.

CRYSTAL CT.

MARSTER STREET

LEONARD PARK

STEERE TRAIL

CENTRAL AVENUE

The northwestern part of Maplewright is shown in more detail on page iv; the southwestern, on page v; the northeastern, on page vi; and the southeastern, on page vii.

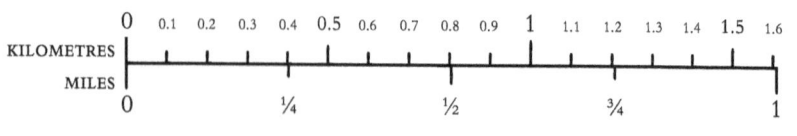

	0	0.1	0.2	0.3	0.4	0.5	0.6	0.7	0.8	0.9	1	1.1	1.2	1.3	1.4	1.5	1.6
KILOMETRES																	
MILES	0			¼				½				¾				1	

MAPLEWRIGHT

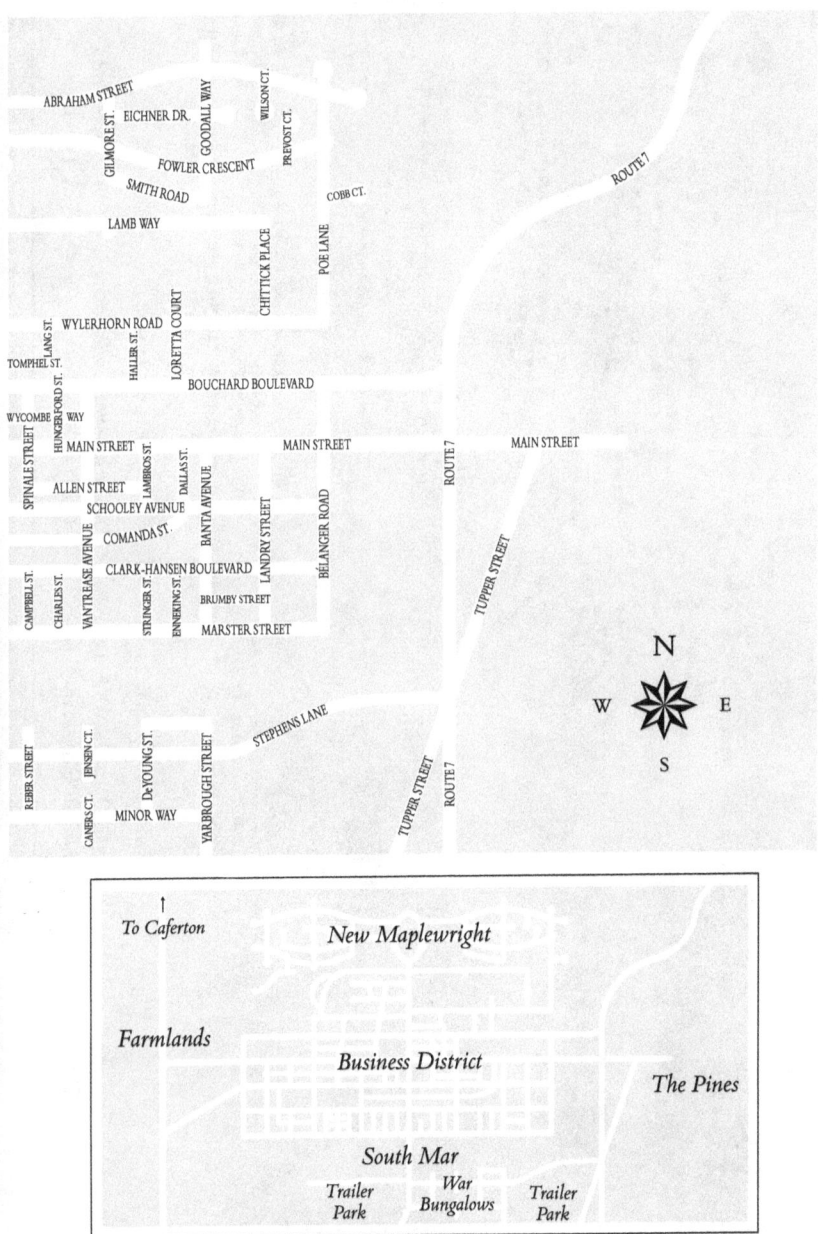

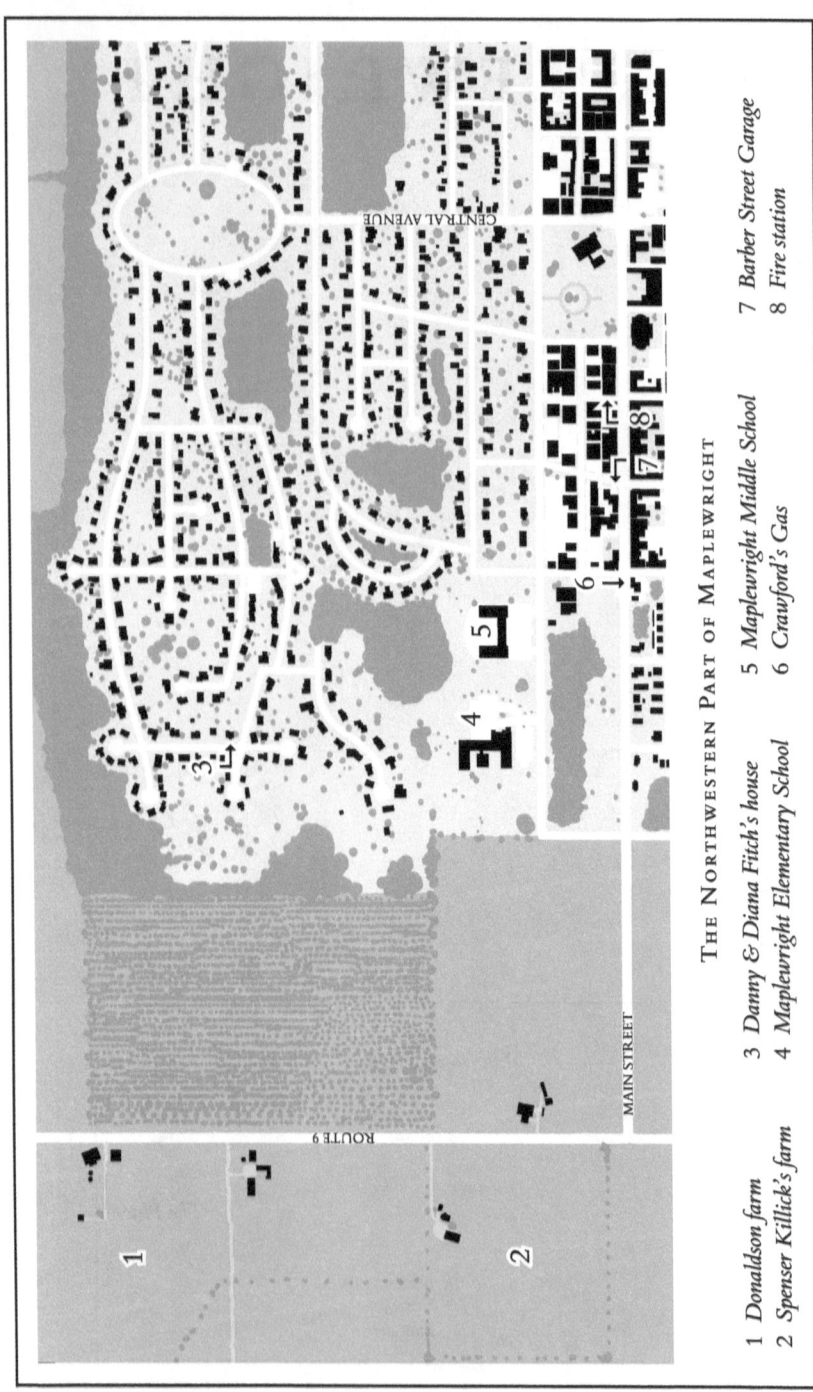

The Northwestern Part of Maplewright

1 Donaldson farm
2 Spenser Killick's farm
3 Danny & Diana Fitch's house
4 Maplewright Elementary School
5 Maplewright Middle School
6 Crawford's Gas
7 Barber Street Garage
8 Fire station

THE SOUTHWESTERN PART OF MAPLEWRIGHT

1 *Spenser Killick's farm*
2 *Abandoned factory*
3 *Crawford's Gas*
4 *St. Joseph's Church and cemetery*
5 *Barber Street Garage*
6 *Maplewright Police Headquarters*
7 *Fire station*
8 *Main Street Diner*

v

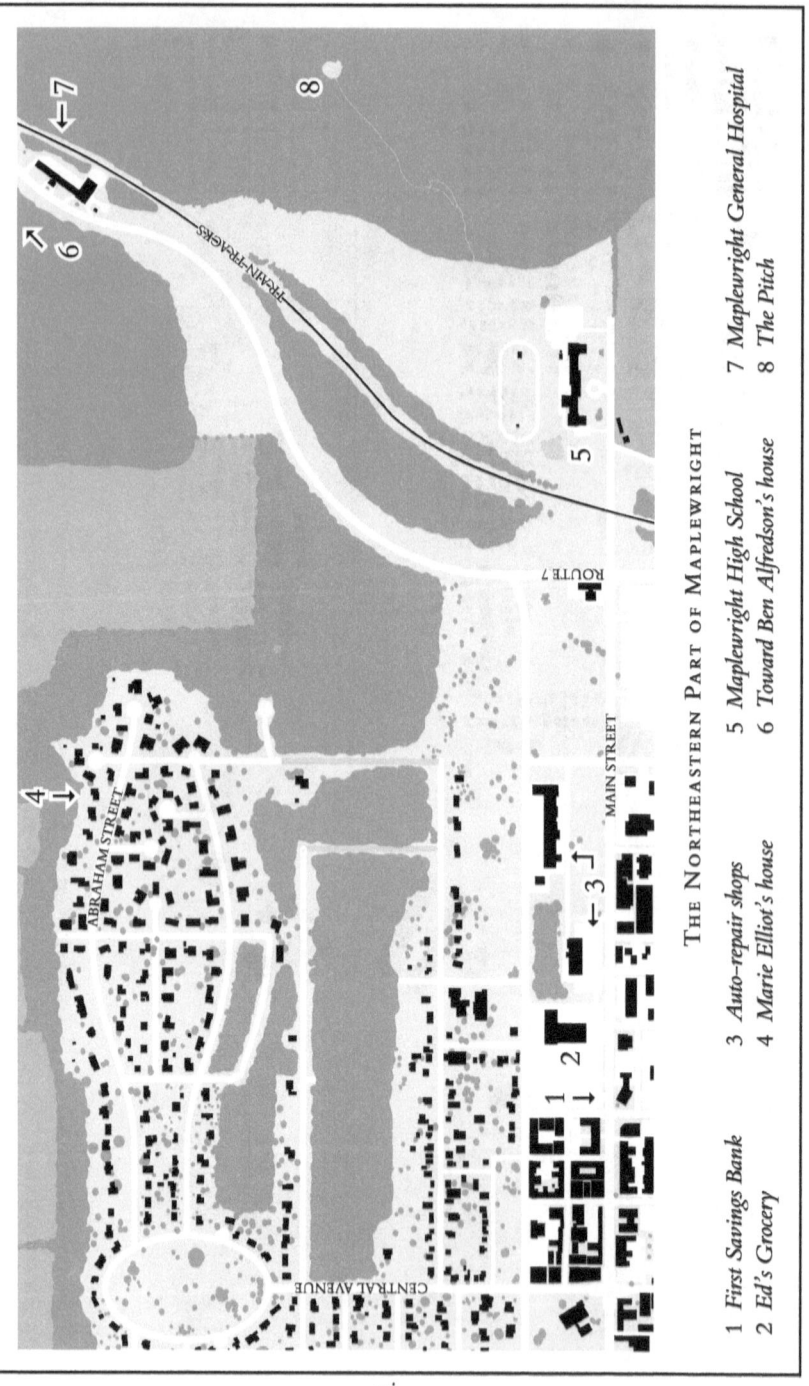

THE NORTHEASTERN PART OF MAPLEWRIGHT

1 First Savings Bank
2 Ed's Grocery
3 Auto-repair shops
4 Marie Elliot's house
5 Maplewright High School
6 Toward Ben Alfredson's house
7 Maplewright General Hospital
8 The Pitch

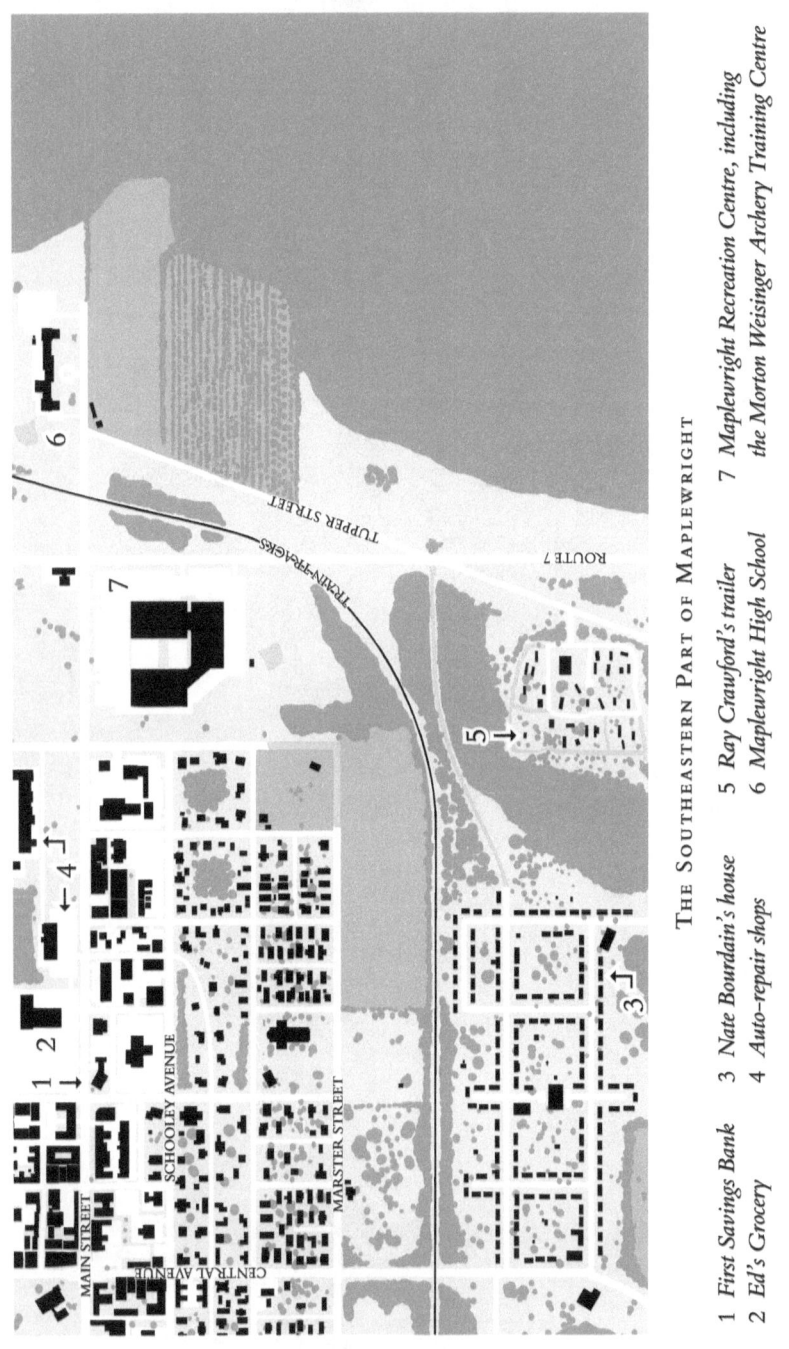

THE SOUTHEASTERN PART OF MAPLEWRIGHT

1 First Savings Bank
2 Ed's Grocery
3 Nate Bourdain's house
4 Auto-repair shops
5 Ray Crawford's trailer
6 Maplewright High School
7 Maplewright Recreation Centre, including
  the Morton Weisinger Archery Training Centre

THE PAGE TURNERS

KEVIN T. JOHNS

BOOK I

CAT & BEAN PUBLISHING
OTTAWA, ONTARIO, CANADA

BLOOD

Copyright © 2013 by Kevin T. Johns.
All rights reserved.

No part of this publication may be reproduced, distri-
buted, or transmitted, in any form or by any means, including photocopying, recording, or other electronic or mechanical methods, without the prior written permission of the
copyright holder, except in the case of brief quotations em-
bodied in critical reviews and certain other noncommercial
uses permitted by copyright law. For permission for other
uses, write to the copyright holder using the Contact form at
thepageturnerstrilogy.com/cat-bean-publishing.

This is a work of fiction. Names, characters, places, and inci-
dents herein are products of the author's imagination. Locales
and public names are sometimes used for atmospheric purposes.
Any resemblance to actual persons, living or dead, or to organ-
izations, events, or locales, is entirely coincidental.

Layout and Editing by Forrest Adam Sumner.

First Edition, 2013.

The Page Turners: Blood / Kevin T. Johns. — 1st ed.
Paperback ISBN 978-0-9920041-0-1
e-book ISBN 978-0-9920041-1-8

Printed and Bound in the United States of America
by CreateSpace, an Amazon Company.

Special discounts are available on bulk purchases. To inquire,
write to Cat & Bean Publishing through the Contact form at
thepageturnerstrilogy.com/cat-bean-publishing.

For Brian and Suzy,
Who were there at the start.
And for Sarah,
Who will be there until the end.

BOOK I

THE PAGE TURNERS

BLOOD

ONE

VILLAINS

*T*he mountains to the east of Paradise Fields crumbled like sand, and through the rubble poured the goblin hordes. From the soot-filled streets of the Fraham village, the monsters were visible in the distance as a seething mass of oily green flesh donning dark armour. The beasts carried ragged-toothed sickles in their meaty hands, weapons never before seen in the valley. For one hundred generations the Fraham lived a life of seclusion, protected from the horrors of the world that lay to the east of the great range; but the time of peace had come to an end, and the age of fear had begun.

The mountains had dropped down into the ground as if a god-like hangman had pulled the lever of an invisible gallows. The deafening roar echoed through the valley as a death knell for Takim and his people. The floor of the valley shook, and the distant sky turned

I

turquoise and ginger as angry clouds spat forth coloured veins of lightning, which struck down at the land with resonant snaps.

"Take arms, if you are able!" cried Takim, unfurling his wings and thrusting J'Gros, the virgin blade, into the air as he sprinted through the village streets. "To the rest, seek cover!"

The market had the scent of a fire pit on the morning after a great ceremonial sacrifice. Women, turned grey by dust, searched for missing children, while men desperately rummaged cellars and unlocked ancient chests, retrieving weapons that had been passed down from fathers' fathers' fathers without ever tasting a drop of enemy blood. Not a Frahman took to the air, for the thick vapours of crushed rock eddied through the sky.

Branna exited a shop, rushing out onto the street with sword in hand and shield at his side. He called to his friend: "Takim, where is it we gather, and how many are we strong?"

"I know not our numbers," said Takim, continuing swiftly with Branna at his side. "But we gather in the Reckoning Hall."

"You go there now?"

"No. First, I must see to my kin."

Branna nodded. "Give her my love. She is like a sister to me as well."

"I know it."

"In the Hall we shall meet, and on the battlefield we will learn of our true selves. Take care, dear friend."

They placed hands upon each other's shoulders in solidarity and *friendship. Then Branna joined the other warriors on their way to the hall.*

Takim dashed through the market at a quickening pace, passing overturned carts and upset baskets. Upon arriving at his destination, he felt sickened, though not surprised, to find the stall occupied.

His sister, Takeh, handed baked rolls and handfuls of berries to those who had not yet found shelter, and those on their way to battle. Blood soaked the kerchief wrapped about her head.

"Take all that you can carry," she said, filling a young boy's hands. "Then move indoors!"

"Takeh," said Takim, coming abreast of the stall, "you are injured."

"It is nothing," she said, continuing to hand out provisions.

"You must take cover now."

She gazed on him with steely eyes.

"Brother, fifteen summers have we shared. In all that time, have ever I followed your orders?"

"Never."

"And I'll not start this day. I'll not hide away behind closed doors and shuttered windows while empty hands pass by my stall. And, when I no longer have fruit or bread to give to my people, I'll take up a shield and sword, and fight beside my brother in the eastern fields."

He felt great pride in her then, but not enough to chase back the fear that rose up within him when a flesh-hungry battle roar rolled down into the valley and through the village.

Takeh's eyes grew wide. "What is that?"

"It is the Gorah of legend," said Takim. "The Gumrahieme, the goblin army of the east."

"Yet that is not what you fear." Takeh knew her brother's face well.

"No. I fear not the dirty emerald men of legend. It is something else that makes my sword heavy and my armour rattle."

"The rumours . . . the rumours are true?"

No one could say when the susurrations had begun. Simple hushed phrases and murmurs of nervous supposition sprang up in all parts of the valley at once. From mead hall to homestead, none were immune to the strange words in the night. Some dismissed the rumours as superstition, others insisted they were the work of camorran anarchists to the north, but Takim knew from the beginning that the words being passed amongst his brethren were undeniably and horribly true. He could feel it in his blood.

"Yes," said Takim, though it pained him to tell her so, "the rumours are true."

His sister followed his eyes to the east, past the pillaging army drawing steadily closer, to the distant and unknown lands that lay beyond where the mountains had stood since the dawn of time.

Takim said the words aloud.

"The Dark Wizard is coming."

Nate Bourdain peered up from his dog-eared copy of *Paradise Fields*. The early afternoon sun lit the classroom with autumn's glow, and the clock on the wall did not tick.

The unmoving hands of the clock seemed appropriate, given that Nate's home town, Maplewright, was a place frozen in time, untouched by the displeasing nudge of progress. At Chip Crawford's gas station, in the west end, the boys still pumped gas, and girls worked the cash, and never the two should mix. Anyone spotted on Main Street with skin that wasn't white was glowered at with distrust; and every gay kid in Maplewright was still in the closet, and would stay there for another hundred years if the locals had their way. Nate hated the town with a tooth-grinding, nose-bleeding passion.

The previous evening, Maplewright's decrepit power grid had suffered a massive surge. According to hallway gossip, the resulting blackout consumed a full three-block radius around Maplewright High School, the two-storey, red-brick building, in the east end of town, just off Tupper Street. At Principal Barks's direction, the school's teachers persevered despite the lack of electricity, lecturing at length without so much as a video presentation or an overhead projector.

Nate had flunked grade three, thanks in large part to his parents' divorce, and he had hated school ever since. It was the third Monday of October, and Mondays were always bad, but the blackout had transformed an otherwise endurable test of patience into a gruelling death march. Given the choice, he would've gladly taken on the vicious goblin hordes of *Paradise Fields* single-handed, rather than face one more lecture from yet another mediocre small-town teacher working in a school where the graduating class totalled less than a dozen each year because everyone else dropped out to work on a farm or get ready to qualify for welfare.

"Blood doesn't just deliver oxygen and nutrients to our cells," said Mr. Patterson, the grade-nine biology teacher at the front of the classroom. "It also transports metabolic waste products away from them. It's a reciprocal process. There's a give and take. The waste products include carbon dioxide, lactic acid, . . . "

The biology teacher prattled on as if performing for a spellbound audience. In reality, he spoke to a mob of glassy-eyed and half-dead zombie teens with mouths agape and minds wandering. While he lectured on blood, they daydreamed of video games, first dates, or a quick death to free them from high-school biology lectures.

Only *Paradise Fields* kept Nate from falling into the same catatonic coma of boredom that had hold of his peers. He doubted that the textbook that hid his novel fooled the instructor; but Mr. Patterson, like most of the teachers at Maplewright High, had already written him off as a lost cause. All Nate wanted was to be left alone; and Mr. Patterson seemed happy to oblige, as long as the teen kept his mouth shut and conducted his recreational reading in a clandestine manner.

" . . . the circulatory system and the heart itself . . . "

Nate had tuned the teacher back out and was prepared to return to Takim and the world of *Paradise Fields*, when Principal Barks, looking especially ill at ease, poked his bald head in to the room and hurriedly announced that the period had ended and it was time to move on to the next class. With the school bell and the P.A. system not functioning because of the black out, he had taken it upon himself to make the announcement personally to each class every hour. He mopped at his sweaty brow, and then rushed off to the next classroom.

Freed from their comas, the students began to pack up. Nate had run out of time to finish the chapter, but he had read *Paradise Fields* before. He stacked the novel on top of his textbooks and headed out of the room with the rest of his classmates.

The forced-air heating had gone down with everything else electrical. Stale air filled the hallways, lingering with the beams of sunlight that slid into the corridors from classroom windows and the school's central stairwell. Earlier that day, the batteries of the auxiliary lighting, mounted at regular intervals high on the hallway walls, had given their last. Nate felt similarly drained.

Ahead of him, over by the lockers, Danny Fitch and Spenser Killick were in some sort of argument. It drove Nate crazy when they stood next to each other like that, especially in front of *his* locker. Danny's narrow face and lanky frame threw alpine shadows over Spenser's squashed nose and chunky figure. They had the appearance of some sort of old-time comedy duo, with each boy's distinguishing faults exaggerated by the other's physical traits. It made them the perfect target for ridicule. They were Nate's two best friends, but even he had to admit that when they stood next to each other they looked exactly like the number ten.

"Okay, okay, we'll let Nate settle it," said Danny, as Nate approached.

"Settle what?"

"Who would win in a fight between a zombie and a leprechaun?" asked Spenser.

"Are you kidding me?" said Nate.

"No." Spenser shook his head, emphasizing just how serious he was.

"*That's* what you're arguing about? The two of you are standing here in front of my locker *arguing* about who would win in a fight between a zombie and leprechaun?"

Danny and Spenser nodded earnestly.

"Do you realize how stupid that is?" said Nate. "It's not even a question. The leprechaun would win every time. Hands down."

"Boom!" Danny threw his arms up in victorious celebration.

"Really?" said Spenser. "You're taking his side?"

"It's not about choosing sides," said Nate. "Those little bastards are vicious."

Danny took a peek at the stack of books in Nate's hands and raised his eyebrows. "Speaking of vicious, are you ready for the meeting?"

"Oh, I'm ready. Things are going to get *dark*," said Nate with a roguish smile. "What about you, Spenser?"

The teen smiled enthusiastically. "I'm not gonna miss this one. Besides, it's Danny who's always missing meetings, not me."

"Come on! I only missed that one meeting because . . . "

Danny and Spenser were back into it, but Nate had stopped listening. Something had attracted his attention. He turned and began to journey down the hall away from them, as if in a daze.

"Where's he going?" asked Spenser.

"You don't want to know," said Danny.

"Oh, God," said Spenser. "Don't do it, Nate. Please,

don't do it. Not today."

"Seriously, man, just leave her alone," said Danny.

Nate ignored his friends.

He'd caught a glimpse of Jeannine Michaud. Dark-haired and large-eyed, she wore a tight purple top with a dipping neckline. Her short skirt hugged the curves of her hips just right, and even turned translucent when the natural sunlight caught her at just the right angle. Nate was drawn towards her as though she were the punctuation at the end of his sentence.

"Did you see Mister Barks doing his whole human-school-bell routine?" said Jeannine to a friend pulling books from the locker next to her. "God, just send us home already, right?"

Jeannine's locker was just a little way down the hall from Nate's own, making it impossible to ignore her between classes. She exuded a radiant beauty of mysterious splendour that had captured his imagination and taken up a comfortable residence in his soul. To consider her was to feel the surging pressure of a world now swollen with possibility and wonder. Despite his efforts to resist the attraction, he could no longer think of her as just another student. Jeannine Michaud had become something mythic in his mind, more a goddess than a high-school senior. He pictured her ruling ancient kingdoms in exotic lands where dragons roamed the hillsides and unworthy peasants knelt at her feet in dutiful worship.

He had almost reached her, when a hand fell firmly on his shoulder, and a voice, from behind, growled, "You're freakin' *dead*, Bourdain."

His body was spun around, involuntarily, just before a fist connected with his face.

Nate felt hardly any pain, only an out-of-body sense of having entered another dimension, where everything moved in slow motion. His head snapped back and a stream of blood erupted from his lip. The sanguineous liquid flew through the air like a crimson streamer riding the wind. The long, narrow hallway, free from the electrical hum of the lights and heating, amplified the meat-on-meat smack of the punch, and the blood splattered up against the lockers behind him with a sickening slap.

Nate collapsed to the floor. Books spilled from his hands and scattered at the feet of his assailant: Tony "Touchdown" Thompson. With balled fists at the ready and veins visibly pulsating in his neck, the twelfth-grader glared down at Nate.

"What did I tell you about talking to my girlfriend?" said Touchdown through clenched teeth.

In comic books and novels, the hero always had a witty comeback ready to cut down the villain in situations like this.

Nate, however, had no such witticism prepared, and was still trying to get his bearings when Touchdown's foot buried itself in his abdomen.

The growing crowd of onlookers let out a collective "Oh!" as the pain arrived sharp and fierce, radiating up from Nate's gut. He rolled over onto his side and curled his knees toward his chest. Blood and saliva dripped from his mouth in a thick, wet stream.

"You think I care about your orphan sob story?" said Touchdown, as Nate remained foetus-like on the floor before him. "You think, just because your mom died, I'm gonna let South Mar trash like you chat up my girl? Not gonna happen, Bourdain: this is my school."

Touchdown prepared to deliver another kick, but Danny Fitch cried, "Stop it!" and the crowd drew in a shocked gasp.

Touchdown spun quickly and pounced towards Danny like a ravenous beast. They were almost the same height, both reaching the six-foot mark, but Touchdown had seventy-five pounds on Danny—most of it muscle. The skinny teen shrank back instantly.

"Don't say anything. Don't get us involved," whispered Spenser Killick, his hand instinctually going to the gold watch on his wrist in a protective gesture.

Nate watched from the floor, fighting to regain his breath,

as Touchdown grabbed a fistful of Danny's shirt.

"What was that?" said Touchdown. "It sounded like you wanted to give me some orders? Is that right? You want to tell me what to do in my hallway?"

"N-no . . . " stammered Danny. "I . . . I didn't say anything."

"That's what I thought," said Touchdown, releasing Danny and turning his attention back to Nate. "You know, Bourdain, you and your friends are gonna have to learn to keep your mouths shut, if you want to live to see grade ten."

Touchdown turned his threatening gaze to Spenser. "That means *you* too."

The blood drained from Spenser's chubby face, and it looked as if he were about to vomit. Down the hallway, behind Spenser and the rest of the crowd, Mr. Patterson exited his classroom. He glanced towards the gathering of students just as Nate peered up. They locked eyes, and the teacher froze. Nate could see Mr. Patterson working the scene over in his mind: Touchdown Thompson, the school's prize football hero, standing with fists clenched over a bloodied and grounded grade-nine good-for-nothing Nate Bourdain. For a moment, Nate thought Mr. Patterson would step forward and intervene, saving him from further pain and humiliation: but he should have known better—things didn't work that way in a town like Maplewright.

Even with their eyes still locked, the teacher erased the entire scene from his mind, as if it had never happened, as if Nate had never existed at all.

Mr. Patterson retreated swiftly into his classroom. He shut the door, just as Touchdown delivered another kick to the ribs. Nate writhed in the pain. Touchdown hawked a loogie up from his lungs and spat the thick gob of phlegm down into Nate's hair. The crowd let out a disgusted groan.

"Don't come near her again," said Touchdown.

With that, he strode off down the hall, Jeanne on his arm, like a prize fighter making his way back to the dressing-room after a knockout bout.

The crowd began to disperse. The fight—if you could call it that—had ended, leaving nothing to see but a loser minor-niner with a fat lip, hardly worth a second glance.

One student, a ninth-grader named Marie Elliot, lingered a little longer than the rest. She raised her eyebrows to Danny, asking, without saying a word, what she could do to help. Silent like her, he shook his head "no." Nothing could be done. This was Nate's mess. Marie gave Danny a sad smile; then she too receded down the hall, away from them.

Nate sat up and leaned against the blood-splattered lockers. Black spots danced before his eyes. "It's nice to know my friends have got my back," he said, his bloodied lip slurring his speech. "Way to stand up to him, guys. That really sent a message to the whole school. No one is going to mess with us now."

"I tried to stop him," said Danny.

Nate frowned and got to his feet while Spenser collected the books from the floor.

"I saw," said Nate. "That was real noble. The two of you are a couple of genuine heroes. Someone should give you a medal."

He placed a hand against the lockers to steady himself. He felt dizzy, and that coppery taste tingled in the back of his throat. Blotches of deep red splashed across his pale cheeks like furious clouds ready to rain blood. His murky eyes had sunk back into his face, and his burnt-almond hair hung about his eyes in a dishevelled wreck.

"Touchdown said he's coming after *me* next," said Spenser.

"Oh, shut up, Spenser," said Danny.

"You heard him," insisted the chubby teen. "He said, 'you too.' I didn't do anything. Touchdown's girlfriend doesn't even know Nate's name, let alone mine."

"*Shut up*, Spenser!" said Danny.

Nate wiped blood from his chin with the back of his hand. "Jeannine knows my name."

"It doesn't matter," said Danny. "You've got to stop talking to her. You're getting yourself into real trouble, and you're taking us down with you. It isn't worth it."

"And it isn't fair," moaned Spenser. "I didn't do anything."

"That's right." Nate's chin throbbed, and his lip stung where his teeth had dug a small trench into the tender flesh. "You didn't do anything at all." He swallowed blood, as a cauldron radiating volcanic heat boiled in his belly. "For a couple of guys who spend all their time talking about heroes and adventures, it wouldn't hurt for you to show a little spine once in a while."

He yanked his books out of Spenser's hands, and stomped off down the hall.

"What's that supposed to mean?" asked Spenser.

Danny ran his hands through his shaggy blonde hair. "Damn it, Spenser!"

"What?"

"Ignore him, alright? He got beat up. He's pissed off. That's all."

"But we're still meeting after school, aren't we?"

When Danny didn't respond, Spenser shouted, "The meeting is still on—right, Nate?"

Nate continued down the hall away from them, not answering.

"Don't worry," said Danny; "he'll be there."

"Yeah," said Spenser. "It's villains tonight. He'll be there."

TWO

EVERYTHING
IS ABOUT TO CHANGE

After the pummeling, Nate tried to attend his next class as if nothing had happened, but Mr. Lynch, the geography teacher with a comically large and always uneven moustache, caught one glimpse of the bloody lip and bruised jaw and sent Nate directly to the nurse.

The nurse was a robust woman, who Nate suspected had been hired primarily because she looked much like an ambulance. When he refused to explain to her how he had been injured, she handed him an icepack and sent him on to the guidance counsellor.

They were passing him from one adult to the next—just another game of hot potato starring Nate Bourdain. It had been like this ever since his mother's accident. The cars had crashed, and in a flashing moment of crunching metal and broken bodies he'd been transformed from a regular kid into the town albatross. No one would leave him the hell alone, no matter how many times he asked; but, at the same time, no one wanted to deal with him on any level other than the most superficial and perfunctory. After a token effort to address his troubles, it was inevitably decided that he was someone else's problem.

Even the guidance counsellor, Mrs. Anderson, had let out an exasperated sigh when her eyes rose from the papers on her desk to find him standing in the doorway to her minuscule office with a dripping icepack pressed to his face. Even if it hadn't been obvious how his injury had been incurred, the gossip had undoubtedly already made the leap from students to faculty; yet she seemed unwilling to state the obvious. It was as if simply acknowledging that he had been beaten up was in bad taste, and she was insistent that he be the first to broach the topic. Now, five minutes after Nate's entrance, and despite her carefully worded inquiries, he had barely said a thing.

Mrs. Anderson was relatively attractive for a high-school teacher, despite her unfortunate choice in eyewear—but Nate refused to look at her. His gaze was fixed on a poster on the wall behind her desk. It featured a man standing atop a hill with arms raised in victorious celebration. The word "Freedom" accompanied the picture, white and plain against a border of black, and hanging in a cheap plastic frame. It was one of those trite motivational posters that were apparently a mandatory decoration on the walls of guidance-counsellor offices, corporate cubicles, and other workplaces where boredom and dissatisfaction were implicit in the job description.

"Nate," repeated Mrs. Anderson, "I asked you a question."

"What do you want me say?" He traced his eyes along the frame of the poster. "I'm not gonna talk about it."

"Fine. Alright. We'll move on." Mrs. Anderson glowered at her computer screen. It stared back at her, blank.

He'd been in high school for only six weeks, and already the faculty had already begun compiling a file cataloguing Nate's personal and academic difficulties. It was the type of thing a guidance counsellor could call up on her computer and read from in order to give the impression that she was familiar with his personal details when a teacher or a nurse sent him her way. Nate was convinced, however, that in reality she knew him only as "the one with the dead mother".

"With the power out, I can't bring up your file. You're going to have to help me out here."

"Or you could just let me go back to class."

Mrs. Anderson sighed. "Why don't you tell me about how things are at home?"

"Things are great at home."

"Nate, I know how difficult losing a parent can be."

"I'm over it," he said.

Nate intensified his focus, determined to examine every detail of the poster. He tried to block any distraction. Nothing else existed in the world, just the poster and him. Maybe, if he concentrated hard enough, he could become the man on top of the hill. Maybe, if he concentrated his will in just the right way, he could escape the horror show that his life had become.

"It's only been six months since you lost your mother; isn't that right? Things don't always heal that quickly. It can take years to come to terms with a loss of this kind. Grieving is a complex process."

"The cars crashed. She died. What is complicated about that?"

Of course, the accident hadn't been anything close to that simple. Even now, Nate had only a vague understanding of how the car carrying the Fisher family had collided head-on with his mother's car. It had been one of those cool spring nights, free from rain and ice. His mother had been driving home from her minimum-wage waitressing job at the diner over on Main Street, the Fishers heading to the city for a movie. Investigators ruled out the chance that alcohol had been involved, and mechanical failure too had been rejected as the cause. Strange lights in the sky were reported in the area around the time of the accident, and some suggested they might have been what led to the crash—a blinding flash or a distracting glow causing one car or the other to drift into the oncoming lane—but the source of the mysterious lights had not been discovered or explained, and they had not reappeared.

Mrs. Anderson frowned as she adjusted her glasses.

"Have you spoken with your father about your mother's death?"

"I haven't talked to him in two years. He's not what you would call a 'major influence' on my life," said Nate.

"Who do you consider a major influence on your life?"

"Peter Jackson," said Nate. "John Milius. David Yates."

"Who are they?" Mrs. Anderson leaned forward.

"Filmmakers."

She sank back into her chair. Her hands went to her temples.

"That's not what I meant by influence. What about your step-father?"

"Roger? What about him?"

"Have you spoken with him about your feelings? About

your loss?"

"Oh, sure. Yeah. We talk all the time. It's, like, real helpful. I'm lucky to have him."

Nate had become bored with the poster, so he tried to find something else to contemplate. Outside the office window, a squirrel bounded across the lawn of the school. It had lost its tail in some unfortunate turn of circumstance, and only a small stub remained where the long appendage should have been. Nate wished he were out there in the open air with the wounded animal, instead of stuck in a tiny office talking about his god-damn step-father.

"Nate, you can't allow yourself to become withdrawn. You need more social interaction. You're in good shape: you could be quite the athlete. Have you thought about joining any sports teams?"

"You mean like Danny?"

"Danny Fitch? He's a friend of yours, right?"

"Coach Simmons invited Danny to join the basketball team the first week of school, because he's so tall. He practiced with them a few times, and then after the first game of the season the jocks laughed him off the court. Now they call him names every time they pass him in the hall. Sounds like real healthy social interaction, don't you think?"

Out on the lawn, the squirrel buried something in the ground.

"Social interaction doesn't have to come from sports. There are other opportunities. Have you thought about joining the student council?"

"Ha!"

"What's funny about that?"

Nate wore second-hand clothes and refused to comb his hair. He intentionally gave the impression of being a slob, specifically to distance himself from the clean-cut crowd of student-council preppies and sports-team jocks.

"Nothing," he said.

"What about the dance this Friday to celebrate the eclipse? Do you have a date yet?"

"School dances aren't exactly my thing. Can I go now?"

"Not yet." She was clearly desperate to find *something* he would talk about. "Didn't I hear that you're a member of a club?"

The squirrel had run off and turned the lawn into a square of dull green. With nothing to focus his attention on, Nate had no choice but to look at the guidance counsellor. For a second, he was overcome by the urge to crawl across the desk and allow her to wrap her arms about him in a comforting embrace while he cried out a lifetime of misery into her shoulder; but then the feeling was gone and all he wanted to do was punch her right in her smug little face.

"I'm in a club." Nate shrugged. "I guess."

"That's good," said Mrs. Anderson. "What's the club called?"

"It doesn't have a name," he lied.

For a time, they'd been unable to agree on a name for the club. It had started out as The Maplewright Middle School Superhero Club; but, because of the varied interests of its members, it had evolved into The Superhero and Fantasy Club, then The Superhero, Fantasy, and Science-Fiction Club. By the time "The Maplewright Middle School Superhero, Fantasy, Sci-fi, Noir, and Horror Club" had been proposed as a name, they'd lost hope of ever reaching consensus on the matter. Then Spenser had suggested "The Page Turners"—and the name had stuck.

"What type of club is it?" asked Mrs. Anderson.

"It's hard to say," said Nate. "It's not like student council, or a sports team, or any of that phoney stuff. It's different."

It had begun two years earlier, when Spenser, Danny, and Nate had gathered after class once a week to talk informally about the latest comic books and hit films. By the time they started high school, the meetings had developed into organized events, with themes, agendas, and even oral presentations. You couldn't just show up and expect to chat about the Raymond Chandler book you'd discovered and devoured.

First an in-depth presentation on noir as a genre needed to be prepared and presented to the members. Only then could one broach the topic of the novel itself.

Through this rigid scholarship, they developed and maintained a mutual knowledge base. Danny, Spenser, and Nate became experts in all adventure genres and all media in which those stories were told. From video games to comic books, cinema to novels, science fiction to gothic horror, swashbuckling pirates to costumed superheroes, they knew it all, and they loved it all. Their passion for fiction brought them together. It gave them community and the strength to stand up to a world determined to beat them back down. But, if the guidance counsellor thought he would confess any of that to her, she was dead wrong.

Mrs. Anderson waited with eyebrows raised for more information. Upon realizing it would not come, she cleared her throat and said, "I'm glad you are actively involved with something at school. It's important for grade-nines to feel like they are part of the community."

As far as Nate could tell, Maplewright High School's teaching staff consisted primarily of idiots and morons, but Mrs. Anderson was hardly the worst of the bunch, so he had tried to be polite with her. The conversation was, however, pushing dangerously close to the limit of his patience.

"Social interaction. Community," he said. "You realize

those words don't mean a single thing once I leave this office and have to walk the halls of the school, don't you?"

"Community is an essential part of the grieving process, Nate. It helps—"

"Just stop, alright? Like, seriously, it's enough already. You can stop. Nothing you say is gonna change what it's like to live my life."

"Nate . . . "

"You can throw around your guidance-counsellor platitudes, but they don't mean anything real. It's fiction. It's just words."

"I'm trying to help."

"No, you aren't. You're doing what every other adult in my life does. You talk, and talk, and talk, but you don't actually say anything."

"I'm just trying to do my job."

"Exactly. Your job. You aren't my mom. You aren't my friend. You're just someone saying the things you're supposed to say in order to get paid."

"I care about every student in this school, including you."

"Give me a break. You don't care about me. You're doing what you're paid to do—I get that, but I've heard enough of it."

He stood up and turned his back to her. As he walked towards the door, she said, "If someone is bullying you, Nate, we can put a stop to it, but I need your help. You'll need to talk to me about it."

"If I were being bullied," said Nate, "I'd take care of it myself."

Mrs. Anderson gave him a sad look of resignation, as if, in that moment, she had just placed him in a leaky rowboat with no oars and pushed him out to sea. She watched him drift into the distant, shark-hungry, cerulean waters, and then sink into the horizon on the edge of the Earth.

Mr. Barks finally announced the end of the longest school day that anyone at Maplewright High School, students and teachers alike, could remember, and the hallways were soon filled with teenagers. They pulled light autumn coats from their lockers and threw school bags over their shoulders. No one wanted to miss a bus ride home, or a chance to walk with friends in the afternoon sun. Throughout the building, teachers let out exhausted sighs, watching from classroom windows, as the first few students began emptying out the front doors into the fresh air.

In the school's large library, Mrs. Pritchard, the librarian, carried out the final tasks of her workday. She too was eager to head home. A lone student watched her retrieve her car keys from her purse.

"Remember to turn out the lights, and let Mister Crawford know when you boys are done," said Mrs. Pritchard, before realizing the lights overhead were without power and the clocks were still frozen. "Oh, right," she said with a laugh. "What a day."

"Tell me about it," said Nate.

He caught her gaping at his lip with a slight grimace upon her face.

"You really should put some ice on that," said the librarian.

"I did. It melted."

"Do you want me to get you some more before I go?"

"No. I'm fine. Don't worry. You can head out," said Nate. "Spenser and Danny will be here any minute."

She appeared undecided as to whether she was willing to leave him alone in his battered condition.

"Really," he assured her. "I'm good. Go ahead home."

After the day he'd had, Nate dreaded the thought of a teacher watching over their meeting, constantly giving him alternating looks of pity and concern.

"Okay, then." Mrs. Pritchard slipped her purse over her shoulder and left the library, but the look of concern remained on her face, even as she entered the hallway. The doors closed behind her, leaving Nate alone in his sanctuary at last.

Within these book-lined walls, he could escape to worlds better than his own. There were thousands of tomes here, maybe tens of thousands, and each housed a universe unique unto itself. Every page held secrets and truths the likes of which Touchdown Thompson could never understand. Touchdown might have been a hero out on the sports field; but, in this domain, Nate reigned supreme. The hallways made Nate a victim, but here, in this holy temple of fiction, he could be a god.

The computer room sat to his left, lifeless without power, but he had no time for that nonsense anyway. It wasn't digital wonder and distraction that Nate wanted. No—today he yearned for paper and ink, stitched spines, wood pulp, and that heavy, musty smell of the printed word.

He entered the stacks, letting row upon row of books flow over him. There were texts in every colour and size—thick theses on the human condition, short novellas exploding with passion and blissful adventure, and well read novels with key quotes and poetic turns of phrase underlined with shaky pencil and thick, yellow highlighter. Each book had its own personality and a distinct voice.

He ran his hands along their spines, smiling as he took in the atmosphere of the room. He felt calm for the first time all day. This was where he belonged, within this temple of literature, away from teachers, guidance counsellors, step-parents, and bullies. Only alone, amongst the rolling sentences and endless pages, could he find true freedom.

A part of him existed in every novel he had ever read. It had been that way all his life. He could pick up a book and peer inside, and, if he looked closely enough, he would find himself there, hidden amongst the paragraphs. Most people browsed the library seeking a great story, a real page-turner; but Nate wandered the aisles searching for himself.

Something caught his eye—a particular book, sitting on the shelf nearest the floor in the far corner of the library. Unlike its companions, it protruded beyond the shelf edge, poking out into the aisle because of its impressive size. Instantly, Nate recognized it as no ordinary book.

He felt the slightest moment of hesitation, and then he knelt down and pulled it from the shelf.

He touched its cover and a rush of warm, comforting familiarity took hold of him, as if he'd just arrived home after a long vacation. It'd been in his hands for only seconds, but already he'd begun to think of the book as his own.

He knew immediately, and with an unquestionable certainty, that the book was powerful; but he could never have predicted that what he now held in his hands would cost so many people their lives.

THREE

THE BECKONING

Nate and Spenser sat in their usual positions around one of the library's circular tables. Novels, comics, notebooks, and papers were stacked in tall piles in front of them.

When the school year had just begun, the administration had insisted that a librarian be on duty during The Page Turners' afterschool meetings, but it hadn't taken long for the teachers of Maplewright High School to realize that these boys were hardly the type to vandalize books: Nate and his friends considered literature sacred. As long as they locked the door and let Mr. Crawford, the janitor, know they were on their way out after the discussion, they had the library to themselves.

"I hereby call this meeting of The Pager Turners to order," said Nate.

"Wait, wait!" said Danny, rushing in to the library with a stack of books in his arms.

"You're late," said Nate.

Danny settled into a chair at the table. "Give me break. It was five minutes. I just wanted to say bye to someone in the hall."

"Who were you saying bye to?" asked Nate.

"Yeah, all your friends are in this room." Spenser smirked.

"Ha, ha. Believe it or not, my whole life doesn't revolve around you guys."

Danny's late arrival had become a troublingly predictable part of their meetings over the last few weeks. The boys' lives were changing rapidly, now that middle school was over and high school was underway, and Nate had increasingly found himself wondering whether there was even a point in keeping the club active.

Rather than draw any further attention to Danny's tardiness, Nate went ahead and began the discussion. "Let's just get started. The theme of today's meeting is villains."

"Who's up first?" asked Spenser nervously.

"I'll go last. I've got something special planned," said Nate. "Danny, why don't you do us the honour of going first?"

"Fine. No problem." Danny sorted through his papers, trying to get organized quickly.

Though it was never explicitly stated at any point, they had long ago fallen into specific roles, with Nate as the group's captain, leading the discussion and keeping things on track with a no-nonsense, authoritarian style. Danny was the questioning first officer, supporting Nate, but also testing him when he saw flaws in the leader's logic. That left Spenser to carry out the duties of the loyal follower, often doing his best to defuse the tension between the other two. In a silent acknowledgement of these roles, Nate made sure Spenser rarely had to go first.

"Valande the Lover," announced Danny, holding up a frayed paperback entitled *Dark Wedding: The Blood Bride*.

At first glance, it appeared to be a romance novel. The cover depicted a woman in a billowing white dress reclining in the arms of a muscular man with long, black hair that blew in the wind. They were aboard a full-rigged Victorian sailing ship, and behind them the last hints of sunlight sparkled in a dazzling array of oranges, yellows, and purples radiating out from the distant horizon. Only upon closer inspection did Nate notice the woman's blank, dead eyes, the two holes in her neck, and the blood trickling onto her collar bone.

"Valande is the vampire from Sandra Churchill's *Dark*

Wedding series. Each book ends with his death, yet each new instalment begins with the revelation that he has miraculously survived."

Spenser smiled, but Nate had to do his best not to roll his eyes. Danny always went on about vampires, so his choice of a vampire as his favourite villain was no surprise, even if Danny had chosen a vampire from a relatively unknown series of books.

"Valande targets newly married couples. Sometimes he'll turn the bride into a vampire; but most of the time he uses hypnotism to turn her against her husband, so that he can suck the love from their marriage the same way he sucks the life from their bodies. After five long days of feeding, he finally kills his victims."

"Ugh," said Nate, unimpressed.

"What's your problem?" asked Danny.

"A vampire? Come on: they're played out. Plus, there's nothing really threatening about them, because they're so damn easy to destroy."

"Vampires *are* pretty delicate," agreed Spenser. "I mean, you can stake them in the heart, chop off their heads, expose them to the sun—"

"Well, sure," said Danny, defensively. "You can do all that stuff, and they try all of it in the *Dark Wedding* books—garlic, running water, holy relics, all of it. But here's the thing:

none of it works! They chop off Valande's head, but it turns out he replaced himself with some poor bystander. The heroes think they've staked him in the heart, but it's really a doppelganger. He *always* returns. He can't be defeated."

"What's the closest anyone comes to actually beating him?" asked Spenser.

"In one of the books, the husband rescues his bride. He carries her over the threshold of a house because she's unconscious, and in doing so he makes the house their own. Valande can't get in unless they invite him, so the book ends with a standoff. They haven't killed him; but they have defeated him, because as long as they're in the house he can't get them."

"Cool," said Spenser. "They outsmarted him."

"Sort of," said Danny. "But, when the next book begins, the newlyweds are just skeletons on the floor."

"Valande got in and killed them?" guessed Nate.

"No. He waited them out. He stood near the house, shaded from the sun, for days and days, until they starved to death. Once they were dead, he entered and ate the flesh from their bones."

"That's ruthless," said Spenser. "I've got to read those books."

"It does sound pretty cool," admitted Nate.

Danny put the book back down on the table with a

smile.

"Looks like you're up, Spenser."

Spenser wiped the sweat from his hands, adjusted the gold watch on his wrist, and then began.

"Aliens," he said, holding up a book titled *As Flies to Wanton Boys: A True Abduction Memoir*. "This book is by Sally Winters, and it's a true story. Aliens abducted Sally right out of her bedroom, and the book is an account of all the horrible things they did to her on their spaceship. Everyone thinks aliens are abducting people and performing experiments on them to find out more about human biology, right?"

"Sure," said Danny.

"Sally says that it's true—they're abducting people—but it has nothing to do with biology. The aliens already know *everything* about us. They abduct people, and do these things to them, because they enjoy torturing people, simple as that. I chose them as the worst villains because, according to Sally Winters, it's all real. It happened to her. If it happened to her, it could happen to any of us. It could happen to me."

An edge could be heard in Spenser's words: that hint of fear floating down from the ceiling towards the ground like the first snowflake of winter.

"After the experiments, they return you to Earth, and you have to live the rest of your life knowing that at any moment they could come for you and make you experience it all over again. Sally tried to get help. She talked to the police, politicians, even the military, but they're all in on it. Men in Black have infiltrated all levels of the power structure."

"I bet you Principal Barks is in on it, too," said Danny, obviously trying to lighten the mood.

But Spenser remained serious. "Aliens, man, . . . " A shudder worked its way through his body. "They creep me out."

Nate was impressed by how worked up Spenser had gotten himself. It demonstrated a real dedication to the subject matter. Nate's appreciation was tempered only by the fact that, in addition to aliens, Spenser was also completely terrified by parties, gym class, confrontation, and slightly to moderately threatening situations in general.

"I guess it's my turn," said Nate.

He held up *Paradise Fields*, by Darin Carter.

"I chose the Dark Wizard Marras."

"Is that a novel or a phone book?" asked Danny.

"It's definitely got some heft to it," said Nate. "It's a fantasy novel about a peaceful culture. They live in a valley called Paradise Fields, and it gets overthrown by an evil wizard named Marras. He's a tyrant who uses dark magic to conquer culture after culture. Paradise Fields is the last place in the world where anyone is still free. They've always been protected because their valley is surrounded by mountains that reach up into the clouds. No one can get over the mountains to attack them. No one, that is, until Marras."

"How does he do it?" asked Spenser.

"He destroys the mountains. He reaches down into the land and calls forth the most ancient of primordial forces, the magic that started it all. He brings it forth and perverts it. He twists it, and blackens it, and turns it against itself. Across the entire world, people are made to suffer so that the mountains around Paradise Fields can fall. He doesn't care about torture or pain. The beings he kills are nothing to him. It's like a giant stepping on an ant. He won't stop until everything is his."

"Bad-ass," said Spenser.

"An evil wizard isn't all that different from a vampire," Danny pointed out. "There are still rules to magic: a wizard can be stopped."

"It's true, and a resistance movement is taken up. In this tiny little corner of the world, the last great battle against evil is mounted. The book's protagonist is named Takim. He's Fraham: they're humanoid, but with wings. They're one of the world's weaker beings, and yet this young warrior leads a revolution that almost overthrows the most powerful wizard of all time."

"Almost?" asked Danny.

"Just when it looks as if the wizard is down and out,

Takim is killed by his own best friend, Branna. See, Marras promised Branna a high rank in the new world order, so Branna sells his soul, and the souls of all the world's free people, for a little taste of power. With that, the wizard's reign is solidified, and that's how the book ends. Fourteen hundred pages of battle and revolution and, in the end, the bad guy wins. The Dark Wizard conquers all. The world is lost."

"Man," said Danny, "what a downer."

"That's one hardcore villain," said Spenser.

"Pretty hardcore," said Nate. "But I'll tell you something. Everyone in *Paradise Fields* tries to overthrow Marras using force, but you're never going to be able to beat a wizard that way. If I took him on, I wouldn't waste time building armies and trying to get close enough to put a sword in the old man."

Nate reached into his backpack.

"Me?" he said. "I'd use this."

Nate pulled a book from his bag and dropped it onto the table. It landed with a thud, sending papers fluttering away from its sudden, imposing presence—just the dramatic effect he'd been hoping for.

"What is *that*?" asked Danny.

Nate gave his friends a mischievous smile. He placed his hands atop the text.

"This, my friends, is a book of magic."

Danny and Spenser couldn't help but gather on Nate's side of the table to examine the book. It was double the size of any of the other novels and texts on the table, and even *Paradise Fields* looked small in comparison. Strange symbols were etched into a cover of heavy, creased leather. Dark tans and dim browns intermingled across an aged surface marked by bumps and ripples, almost reptilian to the touch. The markings were foreign and unreadable, yet somehow appeared to the boys like something half remembered from a dream already beginning to fade. The massive tome's edges were worn and banged up, its corners rounded with age, and its spine ridged as though a ribcage lay just below the surface. Within, pages curved upwards, aching to be read.

"Do you want to see inside?"

They nodded with enthusiasm.

Nate opened the book, allowing Danny and Spenser to marvel at the intricate diagrams, bizarre markings, and unfamiliar languages of the yellowed leaves. There were circles and spheres crosscut by diamonds interlocking with triangles and stars. Motifs of the moon, the sun, and horned beasts piled atop one another, merging together with crosshatched shapes of inconsistent proportion and uneven, asymmetrical lines. Marginal gloss bled into illuminated lettering, and each page glowed with ancient inks of blues and reds and greens.

"Where did you get this?" asked Spenser, almost breathless.

"There." Nate pointed towards the other end of the library. "The shelf near the floor."

"What's a book like that doing in a high-school library?" asked Danny. "Why have we never noticed it before? We're in here every day."

"I don't know," said Nate, "but it's beautiful."

He traced his fingers across its surface. It felt like touching a relic from another world. The book seemed to vibrate beneath his touch.

"I think it's handwritten. You know, by scribes."

"No way," said Danny. "Not possible. They must have just made it look like that. It's absolutely amazing; it is the most beautiful book I have ever seen: but it is still just a modern book made to look ancient. Flip it over. There's probably be a bar code on the other side."

"I don't think so," said Nate.

He turned from one page to the next. The parchment had a heavy texture: it felt good between his fingers.

"So you're saying what?" asked Spenser. "That it's *real*?"

"I don't know about you guys," said Nate; "but, as far as books of spells go, I'm guessing this is about a real as they get."

"It can't be," said Danny, still mesmerized by the detailed drawings.

"What language is that?" asked Spenser.

"I don't know. Some of these letters aren't even from our alphabet. Look at this."

Nate turned to a page early in the book.

"It looks like math," said Danny. "What do you think, Spenser?"

Spenser, the only one of them who earned perfect A's in all his classes, save for physical education, examined the page, nodding his head as he did so.

"It definitely looks like some sort of equation."

Nate turned to another page.

"And those look like hieroglyphs," said Danny.

Convinced that his friends were impressed, Nate turned to a particular page he'd bookmarked before their arrival.

"Maybe it's . . . " Spenser fell silent. Nate had opened to a page written in English.

"Is it—"

"The only page in English?" finished Nate. "I checked. An entire book of spells, but only a single one in English."

Nate didn't ask whether they should read it aloud: he didn't need to. For years, they had talked about wizards, goblins, powers, and spells: they had been outsiders peeping in. *Now*, the real thing, *real* magic—that which they had read about but never touched for themselves—it lay before them, waiting to be called to life.

They took turns reading aloud the incantation titled "The Beckoning". Each boy took a line:

> *From one Extreme, unto the Next, we cross this written Page;*
> *Yet these Words, writ to give us Life, are still our very Cage.*
> *In Opening, we come alive: in Closing, we are gone.*
> *Each precious Shape createth Sound, existing not for Long.*
> *But, now, you Sons of a diff'rent World can forever end our Strife:*
> *By speaking Words and making Sounds, you each can give us Life.*
> *A Beckoning these Words will be, a Call from us to thee.*
> *As Shapes make Sounds, so Sounds make Life, and brought to Life we'll be.*

They finished the incantation, and the final words hung in the air above their heads, haunting the room like silent echoes.

The boys' eyes examined the library about them, searching for signs of change—Nate more desperately than the others. They waited, surrounded by the now eerie hush of the empty school, but nothing happened. The moment was drawn out to an awkward length, and Danny began to shuffle his feet uncomfortably.

Finally, Spenser shrugged and broke the silence. "It's still a cool book."

"Totally," nodded Danny. "Come on, let's get back to the meeting."

"No," said Nate. "We need to try again. We did something wrong. We didn't read it right."

"We read it fine," said Danny. "It's just a book. It's just words on paper. Nothing's gonna happen."

"Look at this thing!" commanded Nate, tapping firmly against the page for emphasis. "This is real. Can't you feel it? This book is magic. We did something wrong. We screwed up the spell."

He didn't know exactly what he'd been expecting, but something was supposed to have happened. His hair should have blown back from his face; blue electricity should have danced across the ceiling of the library; the ethereal power that he knew existed out in the world, always just beyond his grasp, should have gathered before him, there in the high school library, and then bent to his will. Everything was supposed to have changed for Nate, but nothing had.

Nothing!

The book, like everything else in his life, had let him down.

"Damn it!"

Overcome with anger, Nate kicked at a chair. It somersaulted before hitting the floor, where the seat flexed and then sprang back, transforming the metal legs into an airborne projectile that shot in Spenser's direction—he jumped back with fright. The chair came to rest on the carpet, and Spenser exchanged a knowing glance with Danny. They'd seen him like this before.

"Nate," said Danny, "stay cool."

"This should have worked," said Nate, his voice rife with frustration. "Something should have happened."

"Nate—"

"Just shut up!"

Nate felt like a complete idiot for having believed, even for a second, that magic could exist in the real world. His life seemed an endless stream of humiliations. Would it never end?

Flush with renewed fury, he thrust his hands forward and flipped over the round table. It smashed onto the floor, taking a spinner rack with it. Books scattered about them, covers bent and pages torn. Those words he'd mistaken as sacred had revealed themselves as secular and profane. These books were just more harbingers of false promises and empty lies, no different from the condescending teachers and guidance counsellors who offered him clichéd words of comfort before turning their backs on him.

"Nate," said Danny, "your lip."

In his rage, Nate had reopened the wound. Blood dripped down his chin, and with it rushed back all of the day's events. Fury and pain coursed through his body, out his mouth and down his chin in a river of cardinal angst. He cast a disdainful glare at the book of magic, grabbed hold of the page with the spell on it, and crudely tore it from the binding.

"What are you doing?" shouted Spenser.

Nate wiped the page across his chin, staining it crimson. He crumpled it up into a wet ball, and let it fall. His friends watched in horror as he ripped another page, then another, from the book. When half a dozen of them lay torn at his feet, Nate raised the heavy volume high above his head and threw it across the room. It smashed against the wall with a resounding thud, and then fell to the floor in a wreck.

"I'm sick of it!" Nate shouted. "We sit around acting like what we're talking about is important, but do you really think anyone else cares about any of this? Knowing about aliens and vampires doesn't mean we're smarter or better than anyone else: it means we're losers. There's a reason the bad guys always win. *They* aren't unstoppable: *we're* just pathetic."

Nate's outburst had nothing to do with the wizard Marras, aliens, or Valande the Lover. The Page Turners were not the cause of his rage. This was all about Touchdown Thompson, bloody lips, kicks to the ribs, and a grab for power in the face of an overwhelming enemy. Nate had believed the solution to all of his problems could be found in an ancient book of spells.

"I'm done with it," he declared. "All of it."

He wove his way through the mess of books and toppled furniture to the exit. At the door, he stopped and glared back at them.

"The club is over. No more Page Turners."

Danny and Spenser watched, speechless, as Nate stormed out of the library.

On the floor, under the overturned table, red blood soaked into the pages from the book of spells.

FOUR

FAMILY

Archery is a calm sport. No crashing of bodies, no swinging of bats, no dunking of baskets. There is just the pure, smooth elegance of the bow, the arrow, and the target.

Diana Fitch assumed her stance, placing herself nearly parallel to her shooting line, with her feet shoulder-width apart. She wore her hunting boots and her white shooting pants, as she always did while training.

She preferred the compound bow, but today Coach Hester had her training with a longbow. Next week it would be the recurve. She needed to become familiar with all forms of the bow if she wanted to win Nationals this year. Regionals were scheduled for Friday, a mere five days away, but her victory there in the junior class had been a lock for months. Diana's peers were no match for her skills.

She nocked the arrow.

Only a year ago, while at sleep-away camp, she had picked up a bow and arrow and proceeded to hit the bull's-eye three shots in a row from forty-five yards. They were the first three shots the eleven-year-old had ever fired. Now, at age twelve, she was considered by all the coaches who'd seen her in action to be one of the most promising young competitive archers in the country.

Her left hand held the bow steady, while her drawing arm pulled the string taut until it reached the anchor point. She caressed the flecking, feeling the smooth hen feathers through the callused pads of her fingers.

At that moment, right before the release of the arrow, she always felt most tranquil. It was a privilege to lose oneself in the pursuit of physical perfection, to focus with such serene precision that all else fell away. The distance between the target and her arrow would disappear, and all would merge as though they were one—she, the arrow, and the target. Diana lived for those moments when she entered The Zone, that intangible realm athletes strive to find, where all movements are in the groove and everything is right in the world.

Today, however, something felt off.

Sweat clung to her brow and there was an ache in her

lower abdomen—a dull cramping that had been bothering her all day. She could sense the other trainees speaking to one another, but tried to ignore them. The chatter came from all sides, buzzing around her head like a bee. Something had drawn everyone else's attention, but she could not let it distract her as well. She had to ignore the mumbling voices, ignore the sweat all over her body, and ignore that strange, sticky warmth between her legs.

"Diana," said Coach Hester.

She could see her coach approaching her in the corner of her eye.

"Diana, honey." The coach drew closer. "I think you need to go to the bathroom."

Dread suddenly engulfed Diana. Quicksand grabbed hold of her feet and began pulling her down into an underworld of anxiety and mortification. She forced herself to hold the bow steady, but allowed her eyes to peer downwards. Between her legs, a dark red, wet blotch had soaked through her white pants.

All eyes in the archery range were on her. Some of the older girls, just a couple targets down from her, had begun to whisper. Their shoulders were lurching forward in the unmistakable convulsions of barely suppressed laughter. Many of the other young archers were jealous of Diana's natural skills and of the additional attention she received from the coaches. She observed now, with a start, that they were thrilled to see her publicly humiliated like this, the young wunderkind turned fallen idol. Her fellow archers couldn't wait to watch her go running from the room with tears streaming down her face.

Most of her friends had already started getting their periods. Diana had been anxious for her own to arrive—but why now? *Why like this?*

It doesn't matter, she told herself. The shot is all that matters. That was what made her different from the rest of them; it was what made her a champion: Diana had the ability to let everything else in the world slip away when she needed to. The other girls could giggle, mock, and whisper, but it was as if they existed on a different plane of existence from hers. That was why they would never shoot like her. She released the arrow, and it struck the target dead centre, just as she had known it would.

She broke down her bow, carefully placed it in its case, slung it over her shoulder, and walked calmly out of the archery range, head held high.

In the changing room, she placed the bow in her locker and then entered a toilet stall. She pulled down her pants and began to clean herself, using toilet paper to wipe away the blood. With her bow in her hand, she had felt self-assured; but now, with her fingers stained red and the toilet paper sticking to her skin, a surge of emotion threatened to take hold of her.

"Are you okay in there?" asked a tentative Coach Hester from outside the stall.

"I'm okay." Diana pressed the turbulent feelings back down within. "I mean, I'm totally good. I'm fine."

"Is this your first period? Do you need a pad?"

"No. I'm good. I . . . just wasn't expecting it today is all. I have everything I need."

"Okay. Well, let me know if you want to talk about it."

"I'm good."

Once she was sure the coach had left, Diana finished cleaning herself. She put folded toilet paper in her underwear to stanch the flowing blood before leaving the stall, washing her hands, and changing into her street clothes.

Shoving her stained pants into her backpack, she hurried out of the building to meet her brother at Maplewright High School, a few blocks east of where she trained. Part of her wanted to rush home and hide from the world, but another part of her hoped the walk would last forever. She knew arriving home would mean an unavoidable awkward conversation with her mother: she would have to explain what had happened, reliving every horrible detail.

Something had changed within Diana, but she didn't feel

any different. She had hit the target, just as she always did. The October breeze felt the same against her skin, and the sun setting on the horizon appeared to be the same sun she had watched descend into night her entire life. The world had not changed.

She reached the school, but didn't see her brother in their usual meeting place out front. A quick glance around and she spotted him on the far side of the parking-lot, over by the dumpsters.

"Danny!" she shouted.

He closed a heavy dumpster lid and jogged over to her, where his height towered over hers, despite his being only a year and a half older.

"Hey, Little Sis."

"What were you doing over there?"

"Nothing. I was just tossing something in the garbage."

"What was it?"

"Nothing. Just an old book."

"A book? I thought you, like, worshipped books. Why would you throw it out?"

"Why are you being so nosy?"

"I'm not! I just asked a question, Danny. Why are you being such a jerk?"

"It's been a bad day, okay? Nate got his ass kicked in the

hallway and then threw a giant fit in the library and wrecked a book."

"Seriously?"

Danny nodded.

"So you were what . . . hiding the evidence?"

"Yes, exactly. You caught me. I'm complicit in the crime of the century. I'm totally busted. Can we just go home now?"

Diana rolled her eyes, turned toward home, and began walking. Danny followed.

"I take it you had a bad day, then?"

"Horrible," said Danny. "How did your training go?"

"The same," said Diana. "Really, really horrible."

Spenser lived on a farm alongside Route 9, on the western outskirts of Maplewright, , where the town gave way to truly rural lands. He biked along the side of the road, passing sunburnt fields. Haggard workers were bringing in the last of the fall harvest, desperate not to end up like those on other farms, where old barns claimed by fire disappeared and nothing sprang up to replace them. The growing number of abandoned homes and overgrown land, labelled as un-profitable for many years and finally proven so in the yield, served as testaments to a generation of Maplewright farm families left broken and ruined when years of barely mak-ing ends meet had finally given way to the inevitable crush-ing weight of poverty.

As he arrived home, the final rays of sunlight met with the dull tin roof of the two-storey wooden barn next to his house, and then died away. Behind the barn stretched twenty-eight acres of corn fields.

At the front door, Spenser usually was greeted by the aroma of freshly cooked dinner, which he was able to enjoy only partly: six months before, his parents had put him on a low-calorie diet, in a largely unsuccessful effort to help him lose weight. Today, however, stale nothing filled the air.

As he moved through the house, he wondered which was worse at his age, to be overweight or on a diet. They were equally embarrassing and isolating. As his friends scarfed down cheeseburgers and fries by the truckload, he would eat meals that always left him hungry—and yet the weight clung to him, refusing to let go. He'd given up looking in the mirror, and stepping on the scale was to be avoided at all costs. He felt at war with his own body, but the weapons he'd been given to wage the battle were useless.

Spenser found his mother in the living-room with the

television off. She sat on the couch with her hands resting in her lap and her eyes puffy and bloodshot. For the first time ever, he noticed her aging. Her hair was thinner than when he was a boy, and streaks of grey had set in. The creases sneaking out from the corners of her eyes were deeper than in the past.

"What is it?" he asked. "What's wrong?"

"Spenser," responded Mrs. Killick. "We need to talk."

The house had taken on an eerie silence. His home felt too quiet. Spenser gently fingered the gold watch on his wrist.

His father had given him the watch as a present on the first day of high school, just as *his* father had given it to him on *his* first day of grade nine. It had a simple, round face, bold numbers, a thick crown, and broad hands. The only wristwatch his grandfather owned his entire life had been passed down to Spenser's father, and now to Spenser, as a rare heirloom in a farm family where most of the treasured items were things like a solid sledge hammer with a head that stayed on and a tractor that ran even in the dead of winter.

"Where's Dad? Is he out in the fields?"

"Spenser, come sit over here next to me." She motioned to the space on the couch next to her.

He stood there for a moment, feeling like an actor in a play who had forgotten his lines mid-performance. His arms hung lifeless at his sides, with the weight of the watch pulling on his wrist. When finally he crossed the room to her and sat down, he was surprised to discover that anticipatory tears had already begun to drip from his eyes. He didn't know exactly what had happened, but he knew something terrible had taken hold of his family home. Everything felt wrong.

"Where is he? Where's Dad?"

"You know that your father and I have been having problems lately."

"No," said Spenser, shaking his head. "No, I don't. What are you talking about? Where is he? I want to know where Dad is."

"The whole family has suffered. It's been difficult on all of us."

"Difficult?"

"Yes. I know it's been especially hard on you. Things between your father and me have not been right for a long time now."

"So what?" said Spenser, his face wet with tears and cheeks flushed. "Everyone has problems. You fight sometimes. It's not a big deal. Everyone fights."

"It's more complicated than that, Spenser. There are fights, and then there are things that can't be mended."

"It's not complicated. You love each other. You're married. You made a vow before God to stay together forever. Sickness and health and all of that. You're my parents, Mom. We're a family. Everyone has problems."

"Spenser, sometimes problems can't be solved as easily as we would like. Sometimes the solution is painful for everyone, but it still has to be done."

"What are you talking about? Why are you doing this to me? Where's Dad?"

"You must understand, Spenser, your father and I love you deeply. That won't ever change. You'll always be our son, and we'll always be a family. But your father couldn't stay here anymore."

"I don't understand," said Spenser. "This is his home. He's my dad. Why can't he stay here? Where is he?"

"He's gone. He's gone away."

And just like that, Spenser's world fell apart.

It is a small life in small towns like Maplewright, where the borders of the world can be walked in a day. The wind blows in from the west, across the fields where the Killicks lived, into the town proper. Down Main Street it drifts, circles, and twists, then dissipates with boredom, before ever making it to the forest in the east end. With no mall, no movie theatre, nothing to do at all, the teenagers hunker down in basements and overgrown backyards. They smoke pot and drink beer before heading out to drive cars into trees or to cruise streets in search of smaller kids to beat up. In Maplewright, the people proudly call themselves patriots for getting all misty-eyed during the national anthem, never considering the hollowness of a patriotism founded on experience confined entirely to their small-town milieu.

Marster Street ran east and west, parallel to Main, in the south end of town. It served as the dividing line between the southern section of the "business district," which crowded around Main Street, and the neighbourhood to the south, known disparagingly as "South Mar."

Nate wound his way toward home, passing a trailer park and several tiny aging war bungalows, with missing shingles and torn aluminum siding, rented by people who called themselves "hicks" and "rednecks" in jest, but who knew in their hearts that those titles were inescapably right.

After the divorce, Nate and his mom had moved from a half-decent middle-class neighbourhood in the northeast corner of town to the slums of the south. His mother had grown up middle-class, but dropped out of college after marrying. His father's departure had left Nate in an increasingly downwardly mobile family; he would be the first Bourdain in a century to grow up worse off than his parents.

When Nate's step-father, Roger, had moved in with them two years back, it had done little to help the family finances, given that the sporadic nature of his work as a handyman and labourer meant continuous economic uncertainty. A small life-insurance policy reluctantly paid out when Nate's mother had died and the crash had been ruled an accident, but Roger was already well into drinking that money away.

Nate entered the house and quickly passed the living-room, where his step-father slouched on the couch, feet up, watching television, drinking beer. If not yet drunk, Roger surely would be before long. Nate hoped to make it to his room without having to talk to him, but only got as far as the hallway, just beyond the entrance to the living-room, before Roger gazed back over his shoulder.

"You get in a fight?"

Nate touched his lip. The bleeding had stopped. "Yeah, I did."

"You okay?"

"I can take a punch," said Nate. "But you would know that, wouldn't you?"

Roger got to his feet with significant effort. His plaid shirt looked as if it had been slept in for the last week. His eyes peered out over a long, red nose, and his cheeks had the rough texture of a construction worker's wind-worn skin. He slowly raised a can to his lips and took a long swig.

"Nate, I'm not in the mood to get into this with you."

"Good," said Nate, leaving Roger alone with his beer.

Nate went down the hall and into his bedroom. Before he closed the door, he heard the stumbling footsteps of Roger coming down the hallway after him. For a moment, he thought there might be another fight on the way after all; but Roger passed Nate's room and entered the kitchen, where he opened the fridge, searching for another can.

Nate did his best to fight back the sorrow threatening to envelop him. Ten thousand angry butterflies beat at his heart.

FIVE

REAL MAGIC

The light from the alarm clock threw blue streamers of digital illumination across the dark bedroom. At almost one in the morning, Danny should have been asleep hours ago.

It wasn't Touchdown Thompson's threats, Nate's eruption in the library, or even the untimely demise of The Page Turners that kept him awake. All of those things nagged at him somewhere in the back of his mind, but they did not keep him from sleeping. His wakefulness came from an entirely different source.

For years, stories of adventure had been of singular importance to him. Movies, books, and comics—these works of art were what fuelled Danny's life. They had given him fantasies to dream about, heroes to admire, and a moral code to base his actions on. The release of a new book in a series, or the premiere of a film by one of his favourite directors, gave him something to look forward to and a reason to get up in the morning. But all those works of art felt completely trivial now—for Danny had fallen in love.

Marie Elliot played the clarinet in the school band. She carried the instrument in a hard black case covered with stickers listing the names of cities from all over the world. He often wondered which were places she'd already travelled to, and which were destinations she dreamed of visiting someday. She had flowing, auburn hair, which fell past her shoulders; and her blue eyes each had a slight ring of golden burnt orange around the pupil. She dressed with the casual confidence of one who is conscious of her appearance but refuses to be defined by it—she'd mix a pearl bracelet with the plastic remnant of a Ring-Pop without a second's thought. Yet, what Danny loved the most about Marie was the way her cheeks turned the most pleasing colour of rose when she laughed.

Band rehearsals ended about the same time as basketball practice; and Marie lived in New Maplewright, the same upper-middle-class neighbourhood where Danny lived. They found themselves walking home together in those early-September days at the beginning of the school year, when the afternoons were still hot, the evenings pleasantly warm.

They would take Main Street away from the school, passing the bank, Ed's Grocery, and a handful of garages rarely at a loss for customers, before turning right and heading north.

Marie was never tired, never dull, always happy and full of energy. She served as a constant reminder of what life should be like. As she and Danny walked, they would talk of school, books, and music. There was no end to the things they could discuss as they wove their way along clean sidewalks, past well groomed yards and parks filled with happy children.

They would saunter along leisurely, taking the long way, up Central Avenue—but, all the same, would find themselves on Abraham Street far too soon for Danny's liking. Arriving at Marie's house, they would say good-bye for the evening, and then Danny would carry on the rest of the way home by himself, unable to think of anything but her.

He had fumbled his way through three and half weeks of basketball practice, feeling increasingly inept every time he stepped on the court, only because it provided him with an excuse to walk her home. After costing his teammates the first game of the season, he'd been unceremoniously, but mercifully, cut from the team. Now he sought new reasons to hang around after class on non–Page Turners days, so that he could continue to walk her home. She had given him her phone number, though he'd been brave enough to call her only a few times, when he knew that both his family and hers would be out. They were taking things slow, and he hadn't mentioned a word of it to his friends. Neither Marie nor Danny had been in a romantic relationship before, and they were cautious.

Nonetheless, with each passing day, his feelings for her grew. By the beginning of October, she had taken a place in his mind that occupied most of his thoughts. He couldn't fathom why someone so astonishingly attractive didn't have a boyfriend already. When Danny closed his eyes at night, he saw only her.

Whenever they happened to pass each other in the hall, his heart would flutter with nervous energy, and her gentle smile would send a wave of euphoria up and down his spine.

It had been one week since the kiss—seven long days since Danny had slipped out his bedroom window and into the night.

· · · His long limbs made him an especially apt tree climber, and he'd long ago learned how to sneak out by descending the large maple tree in the yard. Once safely on the ground, he mounted his bike and began to ride toward

Marie's house.

He biked through New Maplewright, passing attractive detached houses set back on large lawns. Lit by the street lamps, the avenues and homes of their community held a mysterious small-town beauty. The night whispered of endless possibilities. As he rode into the dark, he felt as if he were moving swiftly towards a halcyon future, rife with pleasure and excitement.

Danny steered around a corner onto Abraham Street, and soon Marie's house rose up before him as a shrine, a place meant for saints, holy deeds, and prayers whispered with hopeful lips, lidded eyes, bowed heads.

With the second floor sunk back over the first, Marie's bedroom window peered out over a portion of the first-floor roof. On many an afternoon, while dropping her off, Danny had noticed that this architecture would allow access to Marie's bedroom window, should one be brave enough to traverse the roof.

He had more than enough courage, and aided by love's light wings he climbed up onto the roof with relative ease. He concentrated on keeping his balance, moving stealthily towards her bedroom window with assured steps. If he awoke her parents, any chance of ever seeing Marie again would have ended quickly.

Having finally arrived at his destination, he tapped lightly on the glass, not wanting to frighten her. She awoke, and glided across the dark room towards him like a dream. As she opened the window, he saw that her nightgown had the soft green tones of chlorotic leaves nearing the end of summer.

"What on earth are you doing here?" she whispered with an angelic smile.

Danny answered honestly: "I have no idea. I really don't."

"If my parents see you, they'll *kill* you."

He smiled back at her. "I just . . . I had to see you."

The nearly full moon lit her face, and her eyes became alive with the reflection of the fairest of stars overhead. The autumn breeze caressed her face, urging her hair into a gentle dance to silent nocturnes. Marie didn't have to say anything: Danny could see that she understood completely.

They spent the night whispering through the window screen. She taught him the names of the stars that night and, when morning finally hinted its arrival in the distant sky, they pressed their lips up to the wire mesh and kissed in spite of it.

That kiss had been Danny's first.

Though it was a week in the past, he remembered it— even felt it, there on his lips—as though it were still happening, as if their lips had never parted. You can't bag and board those moments and stick them in a long box for prosperity. They exist only in the untouchable and ever changing ephemeral mists of the soul. It had been the most exquisite night of his life, and even the disaster in the library had been unable to erase the joyful energy that flowed around his body like a cocoon, protecting him from the darkness that plagued Nate.

Danny now understood that the greatest comic book in the world would never compare to a kiss from a beautiful girl, nor would the greatest film ever surpass a mysterious smile from his one true love. These stories of war, conflict, battle, and loss—they were all trying to capture, in vain, something that Danny now had for himself. He no longer needed to experience it second-hand. A unique magic flowed through his body and across the distance to Marie, through her body, and back to him, connecting them in a luminous halo. This magic wasn't imaginary gibberish from a book of childish poems like the "magic" that Nate had put such faith in. Danny had experienced *real* magic. · · ·

An ugly noise broke his train of thought, brushing away the beauty of his memories in a broad sweep across his mind.

He lay still in his bed, the dark all about him, trying to determine the origin of the sound. The previous winter, rats seeking warmth had infested the attic directly above his bedroom. Every night for weeks, eerie scratching and the patter of scampering feet had seemed to emanate from all around him. He had sworn at times that the rats were there in his bedroom with him, squirming across the floors, squeaking like the voices of the dead. He'd almost been able to see their beady eyes staring at him from the corners of his room.

The noise came again, not from within the walls but from *outside* the house. It came a third time, and Danny recognized it now as a prolonged moan—the guttural, mournful cry of someone struggling against the arcane night.

Horrible possibilities went through his mind, as they tended to do in those early hours just beyond the top of the clock, when the leaves had not yet borne morning's dew. It could be a thief, there to rob his family at gunpoint and maybe shoot one or two of them just for fun. Or an arsonist, intent on burning the house down around them, laughing while black smoke filled their lungs and their flesh sizzled in the flames. Perhaps the moan had come from a crazed murderer, preparing to stalk from room to room and slit the throats of each member of his family before they could cry out in the dark, letting the blood seep into their fresh, white bed sheets. All felt like real possibilities. In the blackness of unforgiving night, death becomes familiar. It occupies a spot just beyond the foot of the bed, reaching under the covers to grab at your naked feet.

Though he wanted to cower beneath the blankets, Danny forced himself out of bed. At the window, he drew up the blinds with shaking hands.

A man leaned against the trunk of the maple at the foot of the house, bent over slightly, as if catching his breath. Branches shaded his face from the moonlight. Night cloaked his features. The dark man leered up at Danny with eyes like incandescent rubies in the night.

Danny had to get to his parents' room, had to wake his mom and dad, had to call the police. He was responsible for protecting his sister from the maniac below—yet he couldn't turn away from the horrid image of those eyes, piercing him from the darkness. Frozen, he could do nothing to help his loved ones.

Finally, the stranger broke the stare, darted across the lawn, and stepped out onto the street. The glow from the lamp posts caught his face, giving Danny his first good look at the man's features. He realized there wasn't anything metaphysical about the darkness shrouding the figure. Dirt covered his entire body. The filthy being moaned, quieter this time, and less ferocious. He glanced up again at Danny, for a brief moment, then turned and took off down the street, sprinting.

All of Danny's fears concerning murderers and thieves, fears that had appeared as real possibilities moments before, faded away. A crazed lunatic hadn't come to kill his parents or kidnap his sister. It wasn't even a thief eager to steal the family computer. Danny had been frightened by a mere transient—just some poor homeless man digging through garbage cans and hoping to find a safe place to sleep.

Danny couldn't help but laugh at himself. It is truly amazing, the demons we are able conjure up out of practically nothing at all. In the night, it takes barely any magic at all to transform a wisp of air into the spectre's murmur.

He got back into bed and pulled the warm covers up over his body. He felt sorry for the homeless man out there on the street. It must be difficult to live without a home. Others prowled through yards in the middle of the night, covered in dirt, probably half mad with hunger—but not Danny. The warmth of his blankets and the safety of his bed comforted his body, and love filled his heart. He closed his eyes and fell asleep almost instantly.

Danny might not have slept soundly had he known that the filthy man had headed in the exact direction of Marie Elliot's house.

SIX

REALMS OF FANTASY

Danny's nocturnal fears seemed all the more ridiculous by the next morning. The new day brought with it refreshed spirits and, upon arriving at school, with the return of the electricity adding to the sense of normality, he didn't even bother telling Nate and Spenser about the homeless man in his yard. He thought he might bring it up over lunch as a funny anecdote; but, when noon came and they sat down together at the lunch table to eat, his friends were uninterested in talking.

Forty years of graduating-class photos covered the walls of the cafeteria all around them. Picture after picture displayed Maplewright High School students who went on to become practically nothing. Ben Alfredson had worn a cap and gown in his picture: now he ran the garage, over on Barber Street, that Danny's father used when the family car needed a tune-up. Barry Hetfield had grinned in a black-and-white grad portrait: since then, he had tried to make a go of it as a city cop, but eventually returned home because only in Maplewright could a guy like him become Chief of Police. There was even a picture of old Ray Crawford graduating from the same school that later hired him as janitor. On those walls were whole generations of teens who had grown up and gotten old, but never gone anywhere or done anything. Danny had no intention of ending up as just another one of those failed faces on the cafeteria wall.

His friends were a sullen lot. Nate scowled down at his lunch with an ugly, scabbed lip crowning a bruised jaw, and dour Spenser continually fiddled with that gaudy wristwatch of his.

Danny had an innate optimism: it was a felicity his friends lacked and probably would never obtain. Nate took everything too seriously and was determined to punch and kick his way through life, while Spenser bounced from one moment to the next, always following someone else's direction, never the master of his own destiny. Danny had carried each of them on his back, slowly up the mountain of life, for a long time now, and it couldn't go on like this forever. He had his own hopes and dreams, which had absolutely nothing to do with The Page Turners. The club had been great in middle school; but they were now well into their second month of high school, and Danny's interests had expanded.

He gazed past his friends, scanning the cafeteria until he found Marie Elliot sitting with her own group, smiling and laughing. Even from across the room, he could tell there was humour and levity in their chatter, an exuberance that his conversations with Nate and Spenser increasingly lacked. It used to be fun to talk with them—there had been Page Turners meetings that had gone on for hours—but these days it seemed that Nate would rather catalogue grimly every possible slight ever directed his way, and that Spenser would endlessly fret about a thousand horrible events that would never actually occur. Marie could be Danny's escape from all of that.

She was fair-skinned, but today there was even more of a pallor to her face. Danny wondered whether she'd fallen ill, and his concern for her filled him with an odd sense of pride. As her boyfriend, he was responsible for monitoring her health and happiness. That's what a boyfriend does: he notices when his girlfriend is feeling down, or a little under the weather, and does his best to make her feel better.

He'd planned to delay going public with their relationship until the right moment had presented itself. Now, filled with a sudden courage, he decided to throw caution into the blaze.

"Hey, guys. See that girl over there?"

Nate and Spenser peered up from their lunches and across the busy cafeteria.

"The blonde?" asked Nate.

"No, the blonde's name is Crystal, I think. I'm talking about the other one."

"The one with the short hair?"

"No, Spenser. That's Kate. The *other* one." Danny was growing frustrated.

"Okay, fine. That girl," said Nate through a mouthful of food. "What about her?"

"Is she new or something?" asked Spenser.

"No! She's been here since September. She's in grade nine, just like us. Her name is Marie Elliot."

"Marie?" said Spenser. "I thought that girl's name was Jane or something."

"No, no," said Nate, recognizing her face. "Danny might be right. I think her name is Marie. I'm pretty sure she's in my science class."

Danny shook his head: his friends were exasperating.

"Or maybe it's Mona," said Nate.

"It's Marie," said Danny, wondering why they always had to make everything as difficult as possible. "She's in our

English class. Nate, you sit right next to her."

"Really?"

"Really," said Danny, unsurprised that Nate had difficulty recognizing her. If something wasn't part of the little hurricane of gloom that circled about Nate at all times, he barely noticed its existence.

"Okay, she's in our class," said Nate, with a shrug. "So what?"

"Yeah, what are you getting at?" said Spenser.

Danny took a deep breath. Why was it that the three of them could easily talk about fictional characters all day, but when he tried to speak to them about a real girl it was so incredibly hard?

"She lives in New Maplewright," he explained. "We've been walking home from school together, talking on the phone a little bit, stuff like that."

"And?" said Nate, looking bored.

"And I guess you could say she's my girlfriend," said Danny.

He'd expected his friends to display a notable reaction to this huge announcement—expressions of amazement, or joy, or . . . or *something*. Instead, Nate and Spenser stared at him quizzically, as if he'd just stumped them with some especially difficult trivia.

"How long has this been going on?" asked Spenser, as if

they were nearing the end of a game of Twenty Questions.

"A little while," said Danny.

"Okay," said Nate, obviously unconvinced. "If she's your girlfriend, why are you sitting here with us, while she's sitting all the way over there?"

Spenser raised his eyebrows in support of Nate's question.

As exasperating as his friends were, Danny had to admit that the point was valid. What was he doing sitting here with Nate and Spenser when all he wanted in the world was to be sitting over there with Marie, holding her hand in his own?

"You're right," said Danny. "You're totally right."

He and Marie were a couple, and there was no reason to keep it a secret from anyone. Long-held insecurities had stimulated the impulse for secrecy, but he needed to move beyond that. They were in high school, after all, and that meant it was time to grow up.

Danny left the table, and confidence surged through him as he worked his way across the cafeteria toward Marie, on what felt like a fateful journey.

He passed a poster for the school's "Total Eclipse of the Heart" dance, planned for the coming Friday night. He hadn't even considered going to the dance previously, but now he saw in his mind's eye a clear image of himself and Marie arriving together as a couple, and holding each other close as they slow-danced across a dimly lit gymnasium floor.

He reached her table, but Marie and her friends continued their conversation unabated. Danny waited patiently for a break in the chatter. They ignored him for a time, but eventually stopped talking and turned to him with harsh eyes.

"Can we help you?" asked Crystal.

"I'm here to talk to Marie."

Kate asked Marie, "Do you know this guy?"

Marie bit her lip as her eyes darted about furtively.

Danny spoke up. "Yes, she knows me. My name's Danny Fitch, and I'm Marie's boyfriend."

A silence spread across the table as the girls took in this revelation—and then laugher broke out, as if Danny had said the funniest thing they'd ever heard.

"Tell them," Danny urged. "It's okay. There's no reason to keep it a secret."

Marie surveyed her friends' smirking faces.

"Danny," she said, turning back to him, "I've walked home with you a couple of times because we live in the same neighbourhood, but that doesn't make me your *girlfriend*."

Kate and Crystal burst out in a renewed round of mocking giggles. When the snickers had died down a little, Marie said, "Danny, you're a nice enough guy; but tall and gangly isn't exactly my type, if you know what I mean. No offence."

The girls brought their hands to their mouths, as if attempting to stifle the laughter, but it was clearly a false show of mercy. In reality, the hilarity of their exaggerated etiquette served only to spur on their taunting guffaws.

"What do you mean?" asked Danny, trying hard to ignore them.

"You didn't really think I would date you, did you? Come on: you and your friends over there are like the leaders of the nerd pack. What girl would actually want to date one of you?"

"But I thought . . . "

"You thought what?" said Marie.

Danny's heart sank. The walls were closing in on him. He could see Nate and Spenser watching the exchange from across the cafeteria. Nate mouthed the words "What's up?" but Danny didn't know how to respond. The cafeteria had gone silent. Everyone's ears were perked, smirks at the ready.

"I'm sorry," he said. "I thought . . . "

His mind raced. His throat went completely dry, tongue glued to the roof of his mouth, lips gummy. He felt skinny and vulnerable.

Why do I have to be so tall? Why does everyone in the whole school have to see me make a fool of myself?

He turned away from the mocking girls, and rushed towards the cafeteria doors. A wound had opened in his side, and entrails were leaking from his gut. Intestines, stomach, heart, and soul poured forth from within, trailing behind him as he ran, painting a bloody path of red from Marie's table to the exit. His graduation photo would never go up on the wall. He would die here and now, slain by humiliation and renunciation.

"Run, Forrest! Run!" shouted Touchdown Thompson from one of the other tables.

Everyone in the cafeteria laughed—especially Marie.

That evening, Ray Crawford worked a push broom down the smooth floors of an empty high-school hallway. The bristles sent dust curling up into the air in front of him like magical little clouds, which he pretended he could command with his will.

The janitor loved his work. He didn't care that he had to push a broom; clean blood from the front of a locker, as he'd had to the day before; or even scrape up vomit from the gymnasium floor, which happened to be the case just about every single time Coach Simmons decided it was time for wind sprints. It was all good work, and Ray Crawford did the job well. Even when it got a little dull, he always found ways to entertain himself. You had to be able to do that when you worked alone.

He pushed the broom faster, the clouds danced before him, and he smiled.

The old man took pride in his job, and didn't much care whether the kids and the teachers respected him for it or not. A handful of the little rich snots from New Maplewright would head off to their fancy universities, and he would never have to see them again. The poor kids, and all those little smart alecks who mocked him behind his back and thought he didn't know, wouldn't have those smirks on their faces for long—not when they found themselves vying to replace him as janitor because none of the places on Main Street would hire them after they dropped out. Just let them try to steal his job: they would have to pry the broom from his cold, dead hands!

He'd watched waves of kids come and go through the school, and darn near all of them had acted as if they were too good for him—even those nerds with their little book club in the library. Had they come to see him yesterday to tell him they were done with their meeting, the way they were supposed to, so that he could lock up when they left? No, of course not. They'd gone home without so much as a word. But it didn't bother him: he'd locked up behind them anyway.

They would learn in time that no one was going to pay them a living to read picture books about guys who wore their underpants on the outside of their clothes. Even the world's skinniest little punk needed to be able to use his hands to make a living, the way Ray Crawford did. That was a fact through and through. Turn a wrench or push a broom: that's how you put dinner on the table in the real world. Sitting around all day with your head in the clouds, reading books about green men on other planets, would get you to the food line, right fast.

Crawford might not have been the smartest guy in Maplewright, but he'd been a hard worker all his life—and just look at him now! He was the king of Maplewright High School. After the clubs ended, after the teachers went home and the last few stragglers were picked up by their parents, the school was his. He went where he wanted, touched anything he pleased. He could fiddle with microscopes in the science labs, and draw big, chalk pictures on the blackboards—sometimes he even brought dinner to work with him and ate it right there on Principal Barks's desk, sitting in his big, comfy chair, just for kicks.

He pushed the floor's collected dirt into a dustpan and dumped it into a nearby garbage bin. It was nearly full, so he grabbed hold of the black garbage bag inside and pulled it free. A twist-tie from his pocket, carefully wrapped around the gathered top of the bag, tied it good and shut. He considered it his own special technique, one he'd been forced to invent because the school board had been too cheap to buy the easy-tie bags. He called the technique "the Crawford Special" and took great pride every time he used it.

He knew for a fact that the city schools got the easy-tie bags, but it was nothing personal. The rural schools always got the shaft, and that's just how it was and how it always would be, at least until those horrible city suburbs ate up so much farmland that good country towns like Maplewright didn't exist anymore. That was where the world was headed: nothing but suburbs as far as the eye could see. The thought made him shudder. It would be just endless city then, as if everyone was the same as everyone else and there weren't no difference between country folk and city folk.

He threw the garbage bag over his shoulder and headed for the double doors at the end of the hall.

Those city schools probably got gold-plated dustpans for their janitors and a layer of velvet on their crapper seats too, he thought with a chuckle, before stepping outside into the cool, autumn night and carrying the bag across the parking-lot.

He didn't get worked up about that sort of thing. If he wanted the perks that went along with being a janitor in a big-city school, he could damn well move to the city. Course that would mean dealing with city folk, and Crawford would just as soon avoid that whole mess, thank you very much.

He reached the old dumpsters and threw open the heavy lid of the one on the left. Normally, he would have just tossed the bag in and headed back to the school without thinking twice, as he had done a thousand times before; but, for some reason he couldn't quite put his finger on, he placed the bag on the ground, climbed up the side of the dumpster, and peeked inside.

"Well, hot damn!" he said aloud. "Ray Crawford, it's your lucky day!"

There was a book lying atop the garbage bags inside the dumpster—an old book, by the look of it. The thing was heavy, and it took both hands to lug it out.

Feet back down on the ground, he flipped the book over, examining its worn leather cover. It'd been roughed up a bit, but whoever had thrown it away was a fool. Guys like Crawford, not to mention his pal old Dylan, down at the dump, dealt with garbage all day, and they knew how often good cash items were tossed in the trash by spoiled teenagers who'd never earned a penny in their lives. Crawford might not have been an expert when it came to scientific reading, but he knew hawking wares, and he was positive he could find someone who would pay good money for a book like this.

Inside the covers, it sure was pretty. It felt as if, staring at those crazy pages long enough, you might just fall right into them, the way you fall into the lake off a dock on a hot summer afternoon. This was the type of book you could take a swim in: that was for sure.

He wondered how long the book had been in there, given that it felt warm. Maybe only minutes?

He scanned the parking-lot, a sudden and unexpected panic rising up from within his old body. Whoever had put the book in the dumpster could still be around. Someone might have just left it there for safe keeping, planning to come back and retrieve it—or, worse, put it there as some sort of trap, knowing he would find it.

He cradled the book against his chest and squinted out into the dark. Barely lit by a pair of old street lamps, the parking-lot appeared menacing and huge. One of the lamps flickered on and off intermittently, like an electric insect trap, throwing chiaroscuro flashes of light and dark against the asphalt. There didn't *appear* to be another soul in sight, but anyone could be hidden within the darkness that swept about the edges of the school grounds.

Someone was out there—he was almost certain of it

now—just waiting for a chance to tackle him, beat him, and take his new book away.

Crawford turned and dashed back across the parking-lot, towards the school, leaving the bag of garbage on the ground beside the dumpster. He ran as fast as he could, the book still pressed tight up against his chest. On reaching the school, he pushed frantically through the doors. Inside, he turned around, balanced the hefty volume in one hand, and used the other to yank the large ring of keys from his pocket. In a fumbling, panicked motion, he sought the right one and slid it into the lock. The bolt reassuringly clicked into place, and Ray Crawford dropped his butt down onto the floor, breathing hard.

He hadn't run like that in a decade, and had damn near given himself a heart attack. He had no clue what had come over him. He knew only that he was safe inside the school and that he felt more alive than he had in years.

There had been fear out there in the dark parking-lot, but there had also been excitement. That refreshing rush of tantalizing ecstasy that sweeps over the body with such frequency in youth, but so rarely in adulthood, had taken hold of him again. Discovering the book had awoken something within him, an echo of his old self, come back to remind him what life had been like before the responsibilities of adulthood had ground him down and age taken his strength.

He caressed the book's cover gently, and made a soft, hushing sound: that was when he realized he wasn't going to hawk the thing after all.

No, old Janitor Crawford would keep this one for himself.

SEVEN

APPARITIONS IN THE NIGHT

Both parents worked long hours at white-collar jobs, but the Fitches ate dinner together every night. They were one of the wealthier families in Maplewright—a place where "wealthy" meant a family could afford a decent car in the driveway of a detached house with two storeys and maybe even a finished basement. Danny's parents insisted the family sit together and eat real meals of actual vegetables and meat each evening, rather than the processed frozen crap the other families filled their carts with at Ed's Grocery.

"Diana, I've got some bad news," said Mrs. Fitch. "Neither of us can get Friday off."

"I tried my best, kiddo," added Mr. Fitch. "It's just not a good time at the office."

Diana shrugged. "No biggie. I can walk there from school on my own. It's just regionals, anyway. I'm gonna win, guaranteed. It's provincials where I'll need your support."

Mr. Fitch smiled, and told his wife, "See, I told you it would be fine."

Diana happily dug in to her second plate of roast beef and mashed sweet potatoes, but Danny only poked idly at his food with a fork, while his father continued to speak.

"I chatted with Barry Hetfield in line at the bank today."

"Oh? How is he?" asked Mrs. Fitch.

"Good, good. Retirement is still five years away, but I'm pretty sure he's got it marked on a calendar somewhere and is crossing off the days."

"Who can blame him?"

"Apparently, the Maplewright police have a new staff sergeant. Transferred in this week. They didn't even give Barry notice beforehand: the guy just showed up with a box full of office supplies and asked which desk was his."

"Doesn't surprise me. You know the way rural townships are treated: it's not exactly like we get the cream of the crop when it comes to municipal employees."

"Can you pass the broccoli?" asked Diana.

"Hetfield does his best." Mr. Fitch handed Diana the

serving-plate.

"Sure, but it doesn't take a master detective to figure out how the pickup full of empty beer cans wrapped itself around the telephone pole on Route 7."

Danny's father chuckled.

Mrs. Fitch noticed that Danny had barely touched his dinner. "Why aren't you eating?"

"I'm not feeling well. May I be excused?"

"Sure," said Mr. Fitch. "Want me to put your leftovers in the fridge for later?"

"It's okay," said Danny. "I'm not hungry."

"It's not a flu, is it?" asked Mrs. Fitch.

"No, I think I'm just tired."

Danny left his family to their meal and retreated to his bedroom, where he could be alone with his agony.

The pain felt like nothing he'd experienced before. He'd been disappointed and ridiculed, felt loss and remorse, often gotten himself into hopelessly embarrassing situations—but a broken heart hurt worse than anything else.

He looked out the window and noticed that, down below, someone had destroyed his mother's flower bed: there was a large hole where a patch of Peruvian lilies had been planted last spring. The flowers were trampled into the earth, and soil had been spilled over the borders of the garden, onto the grass, turning his mother's well tended lawn into a brown and muddy mess. *Typical*, thought Danny. *Nothing beautiful lasts long.* He stood there and watched the sun set. Slowly, it dropped into the horizon, dusk slipped in to replace the day, and, as evening turned into night, Danny wondered whether this was what it was like to die.

A long time later, a knock came at his door, and Diana poked her head in to the room. "Can I come in?"

He nodded.

She entered, wearing her pyjamas, and sat down on the end of his bed. "Can't sleep?"

"No."

"What's going on?"

"Nothing. I just feel sick: that's all."

Diana rolled her eyes. "Give me a break. You can fool Mom and Dad with that BS, but I know when something is wrong with my big brother. What happened?"

"I don't even know where to start." His whole world felt torn in two. Nothing made sense. "It's this girl, Marie. She's my girlfriend. I mean, I thought she was my girlfriend: she acted like she really liked me. But then she humiliated me in front of everyone at school today. She acted like a totally different person. I thought I knew her. I thought she really liked me."

"Maybe you just misread things. She probably just wanted to be friends is all."

"Maybe," Danny nodded. "Or maybe it was her friends. They were there, all around her, laughing at me. Maybe she felt like she had to act that way in front of them. I don't know."

It was all too confusing, and the only certainty was that for the rest of his days he would live the dark, empty life of one who had touched true happiness and lost it all.

"It shouldn't have ended like this. I'm not reckless like Nate, or naïve like poor Spenser. We moved slowly, took our time. I thought we had made a real, I don't know, *connection*. I thought . . . I thought we were in love. Why would she do this to me?"

"I don't know," said Diana.

Beyond his sister, on the other side of the room, his shelves overflowed with books, DVDs, and comics. Those novels never betrayed him. Comic books never made him feel stupid or alone. In film and television he could find hundreds of friends that would never let him down. It had been stupid to think the realities of this harsh world could ever compare to the realms of fantasy, where he truly belonged.

He would forget Marie. He would reinvest himself in his real interests, and persuade Nate to start the club anew. It would be better this time. He would take on more responsibility, and stop missing meetings. He would bury his broken heart in that ugly hole in his mother's garden and never think about Marie again.

And yet . . .

"I just wish I knew what happened," said Danny.

"Then ask her."

"What?" Danny shifted his gaze from the bookcase back to his sister.

"*Ask* her. Go to her house and ask her. Do it right now. Get it over with. Then at least you'll know. Right?"

"There is no way Mom and Dad will let me go out this late."

"Danny, do you honestly think I don't know that you go out the window and down the tree when you want to sneak out? My room is right there! You make enough of a racket, I'm surprised the whole neighbourhood doesn't wake up."

"You're a pretty sharp little kid—you know that?"

Diana crossed the room to the window and opened it. "Just go to her."

A few minutes later, he'd mounted his bike and was pedalling through the dark streets of Maplewright. A new world emerged in this light. Every shadow held strange and threatening apparitions. The racket of the day had faded to the hushed tones of hostile night. The cold breeze pressed against his forehead. Faster and faster he went.

Can you outrun your pain if you pedal hard enough?

He wove from street to street, no longer thinking, just

moving his legs, steering when necessary. Beads of sweat slid from his temples and down his cheeks. He moved with such speed that he failed to notice the old man in the middle of the road, until the last possible second.

Danny swerved hard. He avoided hitting the man, but lost all control of the bike. The front wheel skidded sideways and he flew over the handlebars. For the briefest moment, Danny floated through the air, weightless and free; then he slammed down hard into the road, sliding and rolling across the asphalt as bits of gravel dug into his skin. His head struck the curb, and bright flashes of colour danced before his eyes.

Then everything went quiet.

Danny didn't know whether he had lost consciousness but, when he next glanced around, he found himself on the ground a good way from his bike. The old man he'd nearly hit was standing above him, studying him, and the night had taken on the feeling of a dream.

The man looking down at Danny wore black work boots and a crumpled flat cap of silver-coloured tweed. The cap's short, stiff brim had been given an off-centre peak, and it arched above a tanned, leathery face, creased with wrinkles. Pronounced cheek bones slid outward from mischievous dark eyes, before curving back in with deflated cheeks that gave way to the face's most distinguishing trait: a bushy grey beard streaked with white that began high on the temples and flowed down past the chin in a tangled mass, as if the whiskers were river waters rushing through a set of quick rapids. "Where is your helmet?" asked the old man.

When he spoke, Danny could not see the lips moving, only a supple shifting of the bushy mustache. It gave him the appearance of a foggy hallucination just a step or two removed from reality.

"I forgot it." Danny touched the back of his head, and felt a sharp pain.

"A warrior should never go into battle without his helmet."

"Thanks for the advice." Danny fought a wave of nausea as he got slowly up.

The old man whistled. "You're a tall one, aren't you?" He appeared completely unaware that he was the sole cause of the accident.

Danny went to his bike. The handlebars were bent at a new angle and the frame scuffed up, but it might still be rideable.

"What are you doing walking in the middle of the road at this time of—" began Danny, but the old man had already wandered off down the street, away from him.

"Don't worry about me: I'm fine," mumbled the teen. "Totally fine. Thanks for asking."

Danny began to remount his bike, but as he did so he recognized the long driveway at whose end he now stood. His gaze followed the walkway up to the familiar porch and the front door of Marie's house. The old man had been standing directly in front of her home. Taking it as some sort of cosmic sign, Danny laid his battered bike back down on the ground and headed across the lawn.

Climbing onto the porch railing, ordinarily a cinch, was slowed by the painful stiffness he felt in one knee—but he did it. Now for the hard part: with aching arms, he used the downspout to pull himself up onto the shingled roof. The scrapes on his palms burned, as did his right thigh where a long stripe of road-rash bled beneath his newly ripped jeans; but those pains made him all the more determined to reach her room. The throbbing in the back of his head, however, made traversing the angled surface especially difficult, and he nearly lost his balance more than once. If he fell off the roof, it would be a long way down.

Danny arrived at Marie's window a bloody, sweaty wreck. His body ached, and he felt dizzy and sick—but none of that mattered. He had to see her. He had to know what had gone wrong.

After his tap on the window, a muffled voice said something from somewhere within the shadows of the room. Marie arrived at the glass seconds later, looking pale and ghost-like. She recognized Danny, and slid the sash up.

"Hello, Danny."

"Marie . . . were you already awake?"

"Yes."

Danny thought he saw movement in the darkness beyond the bed. "Is there someone in there with you?"

Her eyes never left him. "Why are you here, Danny? What do you want?"

He felt confused and heartbroken. Everything hurt. He wanted to tell her he hated her for what she'd done to him and that he never wanted to see her again, yet he couldn't help being happy just to hear her voice.

"I want to know what happened today," he said. "I want to know why you said I'm not your boyfriend. I thought we were a couple. I mean . . . we kissed."

Marie glanced back over her shoulder.

A voice came from the darkness. "Go on. Tell him."

She turned back to Danny. "I have a new boyfriend. And he loves me like you never could."

It felt like a knife had been jabbed into his side. Marie had a new boyfriend? *In her bedroom with her?* It made no sense. Even if her cruel behaviour in the cafeteria had revealed a side of her that Danny hadn't known about, he still was sure she wouldn't have a boy in her room this late at night.

"Where are your parents?"

"They . . . went away."

A gust of wind caught her hair, and blew it back off her shoulders, revealing more of her neck. Two red dots marked her skin with trickling blood.

"You're hurt," said Danny. "You're—"

A figure emerged from the shadows behind her. The man from Danny's yard had cleaned the soil from his body, and his eyes were again alive with flames, as if the sulphuric fires of Hell burned within him. Freed of the caked dirt, his long hair hung about his shoulders, blowing in the midnight wind like a noose ready for the hanging. He dressed in such dark blacks that his lean face, all handsome angles cut into stone, seemed to float in the shadows. He placed porcelain-white hands on Marie's shoulders, blue veins curving over them like worms below the pale flesh. The man gave Danny the imperious smile of a killer the moment before he slides in the knife.

He said, "Hello, Danny. I'm Marie's new boyfriend," and suddenly his familiarity made sense—it was Valande the Lover.

Danny flinched away from the window, lost his balance, and tumbled backwards. The second before he rolled off the roof, he caught a glimpse of the vampire from the *Dark Wedding* books leading Marie back into the shadows of the bedroom. Danny struck the lawn, and his world went black.

EIGHT

COLD HOSPITAL HALLWAYS

Ray Crawford walked the black streets of Maplewright, though his movements felt more like pushing through a warm bath. It was neither day nor night; instead, a tepid grey sky pressed down on him from above, accompanied by a sweltering humidity that left his skin slick with sweat. The fog, clinging to the ground at his feet, slowed his pace. He waded south down Tupper Street, away from the high school, the same route he'd taken home a thousand times before, but the road did not lead where it should have. Instead, the street curved before him, eddied, and looped back on itself.

Crawford was lost in the only place in the world he'd ever

known. He'd lived in the town for half a century; yet he could not find the proper route home, no matter which way he turned. Some of the landmarks around him were familiar, but others appeared foreign and extrinsic, as though his town and some other, distant land had merged into one.

Strange images materialized in the fog before him: his neighbours and friends, shackled and chained, paraded in stumbling lines. Ragged steel chafed their bleeding ankles and wrists. In ashen faces, grey eyes stared forward, seeing only the backs of the heads of prisoners pulled in line before them. They were ghosts, though still living, dragged through the misty labyrinths of Maplewright.

Who were the keepers of these good folks turned pigs to the slaughter, wondered Crawford; but then he saw the predatory, green-skinned beasts. Warts covered their reptilian hides, and though they stood like men they snorted and brayed like filthy animals in the hungry wild. The monsters carried sickles and deep-brown whips that snapped behind the queue of prisoners, quickening their pace.

In the distance, towering in the sky and watching over the town, a castle stood, ancient and evil. At its peak, out on the balcony of the tallest tower, perched a figure, entirely cloaked but for angry eyes staring out from the shadows, and watching over the town as a ruler assesses his wooded land before the clear-cutting.

Though it seemed impossible, Crawford knew that if he spoke the figure on the distant tower would hear him. "This is a dream," said Crawford. "Or it's some kind of storyland."

Though that cloaked figure had the power of a grown man—indeed he was a King—he spoke with the voice of youth. "No, it is not fiction," he said. "It is the future."

The voice came down from the sky, chasing its way through the streets of Maplewright, until it smacked up against Crawford's face like a punch, waking him.

The old janitor sat up from the dream, wet with sweat in the dark of his small trailer.

The book he'd found in the dumpster lay next to him, piled amongst the twisted, damp sheets. It had been there next to him throughout his fitful slumber. Though the book's presence offered comfort, the terror of the dream stayed with Crawford through the long night. Try as he might, he could not return to sleep: he was unable to shake the haunting image of a future Maplewright enslaved by an angry young ruler.

The phone rang just as Nate shovelled a forkful of eggs into his mouth. His scabbed lip stung and made it painful to eat. He swallowed and regarded the ringing phone suspiciously. It rang out again, sending an ominous resonance across the kitchen. It was eight in the morning. Roger had just left for work, looking hung over and giving Nate only a silent nod before heading out the door. There was no good reason why anyone should be calling this early in the morning. He put down his fork and answered the phone.

"Nate Bourdain?" said a young and unsteady voice.

"Yes. Who is this?"

"It's Danny Fitch's little sister, Diana." She spoke with a shaken stutter.

Nate felt something drop in his belly: that first hint of growing dread already beginning to spread through his system, for he knew what came next.

"There's been an accident," said Diana, just as he knew she would.

This was not the first time Nate had picked up the phone and heard those words.

A cold sweat broke out over his body, and he was transported back six months: he was on the phone in his kitchen, but it wasn't Diana on the other end—it was Chief Hetfield, of the Maplewright Police. Outside the window, the snow had receded. With a long winter finally banished, spring's first tulips were budding.

"There's been an accident, Nathaniel: a car crash involving your mother. Son, it's bad. Your step-father has already been contacted, and he's on his way to the hospital. We are sending a car over to pick you up. You just stay right where you are. We're gonna take care of you."

It all came back to him, flowing over his body, engulfing him like dark waters. He drowned in the memories, the hours and days of horror and disbelief, that awful call, then the cold hospital hallways, the wake, the funeral—he relived it all, thrashing about in the poisoned rivers of his abhorrent memories.

" . . . found him in the middle of the road," said Diana, "and rushed him to the General . . . "

It was happening all over again, only it wasn't Chief Hetfield on the phone and it wasn't his mother who was dead. Those flowers that had bloomed last spring had withered and shrunk down to brown nothing. Autumn had followed summer, and this time it was Danny who was dead.

This is how it happens, thought Nate, just like this: one moment the person is there smiling, laughing, talking, and living, and the next moment you're getting a call and someone is telling you the body has been rushed to the hospital.

The paramedics, the doctors and nurses, they do everything they can possibly do. They are well trained professionals, who give it their all, but the damage the crash does to the body, the loss of blood, it's just too great. There is only so much they can do. The body can lose only so much blood.

The body.

That's the signal.

When they say "body," it means the person you knew is no longer your mother, no longer your friend. Now it's just *the body*. In that instant, people are transformed from vibrant and complex human beings into corpses, *things* that have to be dealt with by those left behind.

The ceremonies of death, the funeral and wake, are enacted in order to create a sense of timeline. Drawing out the minutes, hours, and days gives the impression that people leave this plane of existence through a series of small, measurable steps, rather than in the blink of an eye in which it really happens.

"Are you sure it's him, Diana?"

"Yes, of course it's him."

There it was, simple and clear. Danny was dead.

They don't make mistakes with that sort of thing. The bodies of teenagers brought in from the night aren't accidentally misidentified by the hospital. It was pointless to cling to false hope.

They had found Danny's body, and he was dead.

"Was it your parents who identified . . . the body?" asked

Nate.

"Identified the body?" said Diana. "What body?"

"Danny's body. The . . . dead body."

"Nate, aren't you listening? Danny isn't *dead*. He has a concussion."

"A concussion . . ."

"He fell off his bike and hit his head. He's at the hospital now. What dead body are you talking about?"

"Nothing." Nate dropped back down into the chair as a tidal wave of relief rushed over him with such force that he could no longer stay on his feet. "I'm sorry. I was confused. I'll head to the hospital right away. You'd better call Spenser Killick: he'll want to know what happened."

"I already did. He's on his way."

"Good. Thanks for the call, Diana."

He hung up the phone and was out the door.

By mid-morning, Crawford still hadn't left his trailer. He'd been sitting at the fold-out dining-table for hours. He'd decided to take a sick day for the first time in two decades. Over the years, he'd worked through the flu and hacked away

a hundred colds. It was amazing what a couple of aspirin and a strong disposition could do. Even when he'd had that cancer scare a few years back, he'd worked every single day of the terrifying ordeal. Guys like Crawford did their jobs no matter what. They got up in the morning, ate their breakfast and drank their coffee, and then put in a full day's work without complaint.

But this was different.

He hadn't eaten his breakfast. His coffee sat cold on the counter next to the dented, rusty kettle.

The night had not been kind.

The images from the vivid nightmare lingered. Ray Crawford was a practical man of little imagination. He stuck to his routine and took pride in the little things in life, like when his son, Chip, had opened his own gas station on Main Street. He knew that making a living and getting by were challenge enough, so he wasted no time on demons and monsters—but his slumber had been invaded by these fiendish apparitions showing him images of his town consumed by evil.

The old book had not left his sight since he had awoken from the nightmare, and it now lay open on the table in front of him. He'd been flipping through the pages all morning.

At first glance, the writing seemed like nothing but foreign gibberish marked by the odd recognizable image; but

the more he studied the book, the closer he felt to understanding its mysterious inscriptions. No one accused him of being quick on the uptake, and he didn't go around bragging that he was any sort of genius—yet, over the course of the morning, the text on the old pages had begun to come together into a comprehensible narrative in his mind. Foreign words took on meaning: sentences and then paragraphs began to form. He needed only a few more hours, and then the book's secrets would reveal themselves to him: he was sure of it.

Three authoritative knocks came at the trailer door, strong and hard.

Ever since he'd discovered the book, he'd been unable to let go of the enduring feeling that someone would come searching for it—but this was too soon. He'd only just begun to explore its depths. The trailer was tiny, leaving him nowhere to hide, and with just one door he had no means of escape. Whoever had come looking for the book had him trapped.

The knocks came again.

"Chip? Is that you, son?" asked Crawford, knowing that it wasn't.

No answer came.

He closed the book. Holding it close to his chest like a protective shield, he went over and opened the door.

An unfamiliar man stood on the worn grass walkway outside the trailer. The stranger wore a crisp black suit and tie; dark sunglasses hid his eyes. Generally, if you saw someone dressed up like that in a trailer park in South Mar, it meant somebody had died. The thought didn't comfort Crawford any.

"Hello," said the man in the black suit.

"What can I do for you?"

"I'm from the M.S.A.C. I'm here to ask you some questions." The man in the black suit spoke in a meticulous fashion, choosing his words carefully; yet what he said made little sense to Crawford.

"You're from the *what* now?"

"The Maplewright Special Activities Centre."

"Never heard of it."

"You wouldn't have." Still the same calm tone.

Crawford tightened the belt around his stained housecoat, feeling intimidated by the lean lines of the bespoke black suit.

"I understand that you recently saw something strange. I'm here to talk with you about that."

The strangest thing Crawford had seen in recent memory was, in fact, the man in the black suit standing outside his trailer, asking him questions. "Not sure I catch your drift."

"You saw something strange. Something you were unable to explain." The man spoke with such authority that Crawford began to wonder whether maybe he *had* seen something strange.

"Somethin' I can't explain?" said Crawford, hoping for more details.

"A light in the sky, perhaps?" The man's head tilted back, as if he were checking the sky up above Crawford's home. "Something hovering over your trailer, or maybe your place of work?"

"Ain't seen no lights in the sky," said Crawford, defensively. "Who told you I saw somethin'?"

The man was silent for a moment. "You haven't witnessed anything strange? No lights?"

"Ain't seen nothin' like that."

The man went silent again. The silence carried on longer this time, and Crawford began to wonder just what the man's eyes looked like behind those sunglasses.

"Perhaps you experienced some missing time? You were looking into a light, and suddenly found minutes or hours had passed without your noticing?"

"No, sir. And you don't need to try to talk around matters with me," said Crawford, relieved to discover they were finally getting to the meat of the matter. "I prefer to talk straight. If you want to know if I'm using drugs then go ahead and ask, and I'll tell you I ain't never touched them and won't be lyin'. Now everyone knows Chip has had his troubles with the bottle, but I can promise you it didn't start with me. His mother—"

"I was not implying you are a user of narcotics," said the man, cutting Crawford off angrily.

"Ain't you a narc?"

"No." The man in the suit's tone had changed. He appeared flustered, as though the conversation were not unravelling as he'd planned. "You haven't had any strange experiences in the last couple of days?"

"No," Crawford assured him. "Had some bad dreams last night; but that's likely on account of somethin' I ate, the way figure it."

"Then what am I doing here?" asked the man in the suit, his face now angled towards the ground as if the answers to his endless questions might be hidden amongst the worms.

Crawford, who'd been confused since the conversation had begun, realized the man in the suit was just as bewildered. He had appeared to be of obvious credentials when the trailer door had first been opened, and Crawford had given himself over to this man's controlled clout; but now sweat glistened on his forehead, his shoulders had begun to fold in, and there was a twitch in his left cheek.

"What part of the police force did you say you worked

for?" asked Crawford.

"I didn't say I worked for the police."

"You didn't?" Crawford was even more confused.

"What about objects appearing as something else?"

"Objects appearin' as what?" Now this ridiculous, directionless questioning was turning downright frustrating.

"As something other than what they were. You were looking at something, but you couldn't shake the feeling there was more to it than appeared on the surface?"

Something within these words struck a chord in Crawford, and he glanced down at the book. Instantly recognizing his mistake, he looked back up quickly—but it was already too late. The man in the suit's posture had changed. Once again erect, he moved in closer to the doorway.

"What is that you have there?"

"Ain't nothin'."

"Rather unusual-looking book."

"Not really much of anything, actually. Just an old readin' journal. Had it for years."

"Why don't you let me see it?" The man in the suit took another step forward.

Matching his moves, Crawford slid back out of the sunlit doorway and into the shadows of the trailer's interior. "I'm gonna ask you to leave now. I've got to get to work."

He reached forward, one hand still clutching the book,

and began to close the door, but the man in the suit swept forward and caught it with a strong arm. He forced the door back open, and Crawford was pushed farther into the trailer.

"Give me the book." The man's calm demeanour was gone, replaced by frantic aggression. "Give it to me *now*."

"Ain't givin' you nothin'!"

The man in the suit surged forward, fully entering the trailer and knocking Crawford down in the process. He hit the floor so hard that the trailer shook, knocking the coffee pot from the counter. The book was dislodged. As the door to the trailer slapped shut, closing them in together, the attacker retrieved his prize.

"That's my book!" shouted Crawford. "You can't take it! It's mine!"

The man examined the book, a slick smile spreading across his face. "Yes, this is why I'm here. I thought it might be something like this."

Crawford's body might have been on the floor, but his sense of purpose remained strong. "You take that book and I'll be on the phone to the cops the second you leave this trailer."

A menacing smile was frozen on the man's face. "I am the cops."

"What? No, you said you *weren't* with the police."

"Is that what I said? Or did I say I *was* with the police?"

"But I thought you said . . . "

"You thought I said what? Are you getting confused, old man? Why did you call me here if I'm not the police?"

"No, no . . . I . . . didn't call you."

"Then what am I doing here? Why would someone like me be standing inside a dingy trailer in the south of Maplewright if I had not been asked here? Do you think I'm the type of man who goes places uninvited?"

The sleepless night followed by a bizarre questioning and now this invasion had Crawford baffled and furious. The dirty little trailer was all he had, and this intruder's presence within it was beyond insult.

"Put my book down and get out of my home," demanded Crawford, beginning to get up.

"You'll stay right there on the floor and listen closely. I'm going to tell you what is going to happen. I am leaving, and I am taking this book with me. You will not be calling the police, and you will not be telling anyone about any of this."

"The hell I won't," Crawford growled.

Without warning, the man in the suit snapped forward and slammed the book down into Crawford's head. The weight of the heavy text sent his skull smashing through the false-wood door of a cupboard. Crawford cried out and col-lapsed to the floor.

The man in the suit's meticulous mode of locution re-turned. "You will not tell anyone about any of this," he said. "You don't even know what is going on. There are a thou-sand different explanations for what has happened here today, but none of them will make you look good. You need to tell yourself, and anyone who asks, the only truth that matters: there never was a book, and I was never here."

The room had begun to spin around Crawford, and his vision blurred. His arms and legs lay lifeless next to his torso. Evil had invaded his home. He'd been attacked by a monster. Nothing in Maplewright was as it seemed. His book—it felt as if he'd had it all his life, even before birth—was be-ing taken from him. His dreams and waking life, they were all mixing together. Monsters and killers, dark rulers and men in black suits . . .

"I . . . need help," he said.

"You aren't going to get it. Now repeat after me: there was no book; I was never here."

"There was no book," said Crawford, his pained voice crumbling listlessly into the floor in front of his face. "You were never here."

"Good."

The man in the black suit left the trailer with the book

in his hands, leaving Crawford to bleed into the carpet.

North up Tupper Street—away from the South Mar trailer park where Ray Crawford lay bleeding—past the school to the northeast, and just off Route 7 stood Maplewright General Hospital. Serving three neighbouring communities along with the town proper, the grey concrete building, with its long rows of tall, narrow windows, was one of the largest structures in use in the township. Nate and Spenser sat on a small bench in a hallway illuminated by the green-tinged fluorescent lights on the second floor. They'd been waiting all morning.

Spenser toyed nervously with his wristwatch, while Nate grew increasingly tired of staring at the snot-green walls. Watching the nurses walk the hallway in front of them wasn't any better: their movements were mechanical and emotionless—they'd done it all a thousand times before. Nate wondered whether anyone in the entire building, apart from him and Spenser, even cared that their friend had been hurt.

Down the hall from them, a portion of the paediatric ward had been converted into a geriatric unit. Maplewright's population was growing old, and it seemed the town had all but given up on producing a younger generation.

Spenser peered up from his watch and asked, "Do you think he's alright?" for the third time.

"I'm sure he's fine," said Nate. "Guys wipe out on their bikes all the time. No big deal. Danny is tall, so the fall is a bit farther for him than it would be for us; but he'll be okay."

Nate squinted his eyes closed, shutting out the world. When he opened them again, he saw tears rolling from Spenser's eyes and down his cheeks.

"Hey, Spenser, listen: I promise Danny is going to be okay. Don't cry. He's gonna be just fine." He threw an arm over Spenser's shoulder, trying to comfort him.

Spenser wiped the tears with his sleeve. "It's not that."

"Oh?"

"It's my parents. They're getting divorced."

A nurse hurried by them, not bothering to ask what was wrong. Tearful visitors were a familiar presence in these cold halls.

Nate was momentarily dumbstruck. " . . . Divorced? I didn't even realize they were having problems."

"Neither did I. I mean, they fight a lot, but don't everyone's parents fight?"

"Does your dad smack her around? Hit her and stuff?"

"No! Nothing like that. He'll yell a bit and maybe punch the wall sometimes, and she'll cry a lot, but nothing violent. I mean, it's just disagreements and misunderstandings and that sort of stuff. That's all. Just a regular, everyday fight, you know? So what's the big deal? Isn't that normal? Don't everyone's parents fight?"

Nate thought about it for a moment. Forced to answer honestly, he said, "Spenser, I really don't know. I can barely remember my parents living together. I haven't spoken to my father in years. I have no idea what it's like to live with a mom and a dad. That's like something out of a movie to me—family is as much a fantasy as wizards and goblins."

"What about Roger?" suggested Spenser.

"Roger? You're kidding, right?"

"Mom says my dad's staying at my uncle's house in Caferton," said Spenser, almost to himself. "But he hasn't called, hasn't emailed me, hasn't texted, nothing. It's like one day he's my dad, and the next day he's just gone from my life. He just left me completely on my own."

Nate nodded: he understood perfectly. It had been the same way with his own father. These men, they just disappeared into the night.

The door to the hospital room opened, and Danny's family entered the hall. Spenser quickly wiped away his tears as he and Nate got to their feet.

"Spenser, Nate, thank you both for coming," said Mrs. Fitch.

"I want the two of you to take careful note of this," said Mr. Fitch, who considered Nate a bad influence on his son, and would eventually find some way to blame Nate for the accident, if he hadn't already. "This is what happens when you go sneaking off in the middle of the night. God only knows what Danny was thinking. He could have been seriously hurt. It was a stupid thing to do. I expect better than this from all three of you."

"Yes, sir," said Spenser. "Totally stupid."

"Can we see him?" asked Nate.

"He's still a little confused about what happened," said Mrs. Fitch, "so try not to upset him. You can pop in and say hello. But don't stay too long: he's very tired."

"We won't upset him," said Spenser.

Mr. and Mrs. Fitch began to move down the hall, but Diana remained behind. "Go ahead," she said to her parents. "I'll meet you in the cafeteria."

"Okay. We'll buy you some lunch."

Once her parents were a safe distance away, Diana's expression changed to one of deep concern. "This is all my fault," she confessed.

"What are you talking about?" said Nate.

"I told him to go. He was upset about that girl, so I told

him to sneak out and see her. I didn't think he would end up in the hospital!"

"No one is blaming you," said Nate. "You heard what your dad just said. He thinks this whole thing is my fault—as usual. You're in the clear."

"I just feel horrible, you guys. I'm really worried about Danny. Something weird is going on with him."

"What do you mean, 'weird'?" asked Spenser.

"He's acting strange, saying all sorts of crazy stuff."

"He has a concussion, right? I'm sure that's all totally normal. I mean, isn't it normal, Nate?"

"Yeah, it's normal. Don't worry about your brother, Diana. He'll be okay."

"Just talk to him, alright?" Diana frowned. "Something is going on with him. I never should have told him to go out." She glanced back towards her brother's room, worried, before heading down the hallway to meet her parents in the cafeteria.

Nate and Spenser entered Danny's room.

He lay stretched out on a hospital bed, wearing a pastel-blue hospital gown. Thick white gauze had been wrapped about his head. Smaller bandages covered his hands and parts of his arms. A miniature television set was mounted on a mobile arm next to the bed, but it had been pushed off to the side and was not turned on. A window on the far side of the room looked out onto the courtyard, where Nate could see an ancient woman in a wheelchair being pushed by a bored nurse.

"You're finally here," breathed Danny.

"Dude," said Spenser, moving to the side of the bed, "you look like the Mummy."

"Close the door," instructed Danny.

Nate did as asked and then joined Spenser at the side of the bed. "Are you alright? You look pretty banged up."

"You've got to listen to me. They don't believe me. They think I hit my head. They keep asking me if I know my mother's maiden name and who my first-grade teacher was."

"You did hit your head," said Nate. "You have a concussion. Some guy found you passed out in the middle of the road after you crashed your bike. You're lucky he didn't run you over. We just saw Diana in the hallway outside. She's all broken up about it. She thinks this whole thing is her fault. What did you say to her? She's really freaked out."

"Forget the concussion: I know what happened. There was a crazy old man. He had this long beard, and he was standing there in the middle of the road, but that was before I fell off the roof. That's what knocked me out—not the accident on my bike."

"What roof?" asked Spenser. "It wasn't a bike accident?"

"I fell off the roof after I crashed my bike. I hit my head twice, but no one believes me about the second time."

Nate and Spenser shared worried glances with each other. Nate had been focused on assuring Spenser that Danny would be fine. He hadn't prepared himself for the possibility that the accident had left his friend in a slightly frightening state of confusion.

"I know it sounds crazy, but someone protected me. When they found me, I was wearing this." He pulled a necklace out from under his gown: a silver crucifix, large and gaudy, weighed on the chain. He lifted it from his chest, allowing Nate and Spenser to examine it. Even in the stale light of the hospital room, the silver sparkled. "This isn't mine," he said. "Someone protected me after I fell."

"Danny, maybe we should go," said Nate. "You aren't making a lot of sense. Old men, bikes, roofs, crucifixes . . . . Seriously, man, we should let you get some rest. We'll come back when you're feeling better."

"Don't say that! If you guys don't believe me, no one will. We only have three days left! We're already running out of time!" He grabbed Nate's shirt and pulled him in close. "The spell in the library—it worked. Okay? Don't you get it? We thought it didn't do anything, but it did. It brought him here. It made him real."

"Brought who here?"

Danny released Nate's shirt and dropped his head back into the pillow. Staring up with distant eyes, as if the ceiling were a long way off, he said, "Valande the Lover. The vampire from the *Dark Wedding* books. I thought someone had ruined my mom's flowers just to be mean or something, but I think he actually came up out of the garden two nights ago. I mean, I saw him, and I should have recognized him, but it was dark and he was dirty." He turned again to his friends. "Don't you see? That's what the spell was for: it brought him out of the book. He's here in our world, and he's got Marie."

"Marie? The girl from the cafeteria?" asked Spenser.

"Valande's feeding off her. That's why she said she wasn't my girlfriend. He's *controlling* her, just like in the books. I saw the marks on her neck myself. Marie must have invited him in to her house. I don't know what's happened to her parents. I've got to get her out of there, but they won't let me leave because of the concussion. They want to monitor me for another day."

Danny appeared dizzy, sick and slightly crazed. "Promise me, Nate. Promise me that you'll help her. Please: he's going to *kill* her."

Nate didn't know what to say.

"She lives at 48 Abraham Street. Go to the house,"

pleaded Danny. "Do it now. Get her out before it's too late. He kills them after five days. That means there are only three days left."

"Danny, you're—"

"Just promise me!"

Nate started to say something else but, before he could, Spenser blurted out, "We promise."

Nate shot him an angry glare. Playing into Danny's delusion would only make matters worse.

"Don't worry," said Spenser, ignoring Nate. "Your mom said you have to stay calm, so just relax, alright? We'll go to Marie's house—Marie *Elliot*, right? Forty-eight Abraham: I know where that is. We'll make sure she's safe. Won't we, Nate?"

Spenser raised his eyebrows, clearly wanting Nate to play along. Not sure what his other options could be, Nate gave in.

"That's right," he said reluctantly. "We'll make sure the vampire that came up out of your mom's flower garden doesn't have your girlfriend, who won't actually admit to being your girlfriend."

"It's real. I know you don't believe me, but it's real."

"Okay. We're on it," said Spenser.

Nate nodded towards the door. "We'll see you around, okay, buddy? Just try to take it easy."

"And don't worry," said Spenser. "We'll save the girl."

They were about to close the door behind themselves when Danny called to them. They stopped and gazed back at him.

"Bring wooden stakes."

NINE

THE HOUSE OF DEATH

Nate and Spenser stood at the end of the driveway, evaluating Marie's modest house.

"Doesn't look evil," said Spenser with a shrug.

Nate sighed. "Let's get this over with."

They hadn't bothered to bring any stakes, despite Danny's insistence that they do so. Just being there to check on her felt ridiculous enough.

Nate started up the driveway towards the front porch. After a few steps, he noticed Spenser hadn't followed him.

"What if it's real?" asked Spenser, still at the curb. "What if Valande really is in there?"

Nate threw his arms up. "Look: it was just a stupid book. Danny hit his head and went a little mental. There's no vampire in there. We promised him we would do this, so let's just do it already."

He continued towards the house and, by the time he had crossed the porch and approached the front door, Spenser had caught up with him. "I'm just saying it wouldn't hurt to have a plan is all."

"How's this for a plan?" Nate raised his hand and knocked on the door.

When no one had answered after a few seconds, Nate concluded, "Nobody's home. Let's go."

Spenser tried the doorknob. It turned easily. No sooner had he pushed open the door than his hand shot instinctively to cover his mouth and nose. "What is that *smell*?"

"Nothing good," answered Nate, his senses keenly awakened by the horrific stench.

He stepped inside the house. Spenser followed, sticking close behind Nate. At their left was a small office; the blinds were closed over its windows, and shadows crept out from the room into the portrait-lined hallway ahead of them. The smell permeated the air—that inescapable ammonia scent of meat gone rancid—causing them to gag, and something hummed softly from the far end of the hall. The sound grew louder as they ventured forth, passing family photos from a happier time. As the boys entered the Elliots' living-room, the source of the sound revealed itself: the legions of flies and their maggot offspring had already set in.

Spenser gasped. "Oh, no. God, no." The smell, combined with this appalling visual assault, overwhelmed him. His stomach lurching, he bent over and let loose.

Two human bodies lay naked on floor before them. There was an eerie stillness to the flesh. There was no expansion and contraction of their torsos, not the slightest breath drawn; nor was there any evidence of blood pumping through those veins: this was death the boys had walked in upon. Though the faces of the corpses were partly ravaged and putrefaction had begun, enough of Marie's parents' features remained that they could be recognized from their portraits Nate and Spenser in the hallway. The Elliots' skin had turned a horrid, waxy yellow, and was pocked all over with burgundy wounds. At their necks were ragged holes, where chunks of flesh had been torn away; and the floor beneath their bodies was wet with the fluids of autolysis and decomposition.

Nate was overcome by the memory of his mother's body laid out before him in a pine casket, lined with cream-coloured satin. He hadn't believed in the human soul before that moment, but upon viewing that empty shell, that decaying organic mass that had once been his mother, he became convinced that something beyond mere biology alighted in the human body and turned it into a person. No child who has buried a parent would deny the metaphysical. No orphaned son can cling to this earth as though it is all there is to existence. Death takes much from the young; but it also shares cosmic truths, for it had taught Nate that there are other worlds than this world and that luminescent beings are we.

Spenser tugged at Nate's shoulder. "We have to get out of here. We have to call the police. They're *dead*." Unwilling to wait for Nate, Spenser stumbled away from the living-room, down the hallway, and out the front door.

Nate left the bodies to the insects and followed.

Spenser had dropped to his knees on the porch. He stared down at the wooden floor, taking deep, gasping breaths, trying to rid his lungs of the reeking odour. When Nate reached down and touched him on the shoulder, Spenser flinched away.

"They're dead," he said. "They're dead." He seemed unable to say anything else.

"I know." Nate knelt down next to him. "But Marie might still be in there. We need to go back in."

Sweat was splashed across Spenser's goose-bumped flesh, which had taken on a lime tone. He shook his head. "I can't." A sudden small surge of soiled saliva dripped from his mouth onto his hands, over the face of his gold wristwatch. "I'm sorry, but I can't go back in there."

"Alright." Nate rose up. "I understand."

"I'll be out here. I won't leave you."

Nate nodded.

He took one last look at his friend, then entered again the house of death.

Other than the insects and the bodies, Nate found nothing else on the first floor, but even the absence itself seemed to carry with it a monstrously heavy load. The intangible lurking energies of violence and death radiated everywhere.

He mounted the stairs to the second floor, trying to forget the image of a massive fly, its thorax thick and hairy, crawling across Marie's mother's eyeball—still opened wide and staring, even in death.

As he ascended, Nate wondered whether he had become the character from the slasher film, foolishly entering the room the audience already knew the killer was in. He preferred to think of himself as the chivalric hero risking it all to save the maiden, but the truth was that he didn't feel like an archetype of any kind—only a frightened teenager trying to fulfill a promise he'd made to a friend, but unsure whether he had the strength.

Upstairs, he moved from room to room. The air smelled different up here, but no better than below. A suffocating humidity exaggerated the musky odour of tears and sweat and unspeakable deeds. Nate opened closets, expecting to be greeted by the killer's malicious visage, and searched under beds, ready to find Marie's dead body lying there twisted and broken.

He wished he'd heeded Danny's advice and brought a stake with him. He didn't believe a fictional vampire turned real had committed these crimes, but a stake could have at least served as a weapon against the killer. Nate couldn't even fight Touchdown Thompson, a high-school student—and now he might have to face a full-grown murderer.

Finally he came to the last of the upstairs rooms: Marie's bedroom. Stuffed toys, comforting reminders of a child-hood now gone, sat in one corner, a bookcase beside them. There was a desk, a stereo, and a dresser topped with framed photos of Marie, her family, her friends. The comforter lay in a heap at the foot of the bed. The white top-sheet had been stained dark red in several spots. Nate averted his gaze from this place of slumber turned hecatomb to one hundred bites. He checked the closet, and then under the bed, but found nothing.

With the two main floors cleared, there was only one place left to look.

Nate headed back down the stairs.

Had he truly failed to notice how ominous the door to the basement appeared when he first swept through the main floor, or had he subconsciously chosen to ignore it? Either way, the door had become unavoidable. He would have to go through it and descend belowground.

He touched the cold doorknob, turned, and pulled. Before him, there dropped a foreboding stairway, sliding down into a black abyss. He touched the wall, searching for a light switch. Where was it?

Finally, his fingers came into contact with the flat surface of the switch plate—but he soon discovered that the switch itself was gone. All that remained was a jagged edge of plastic, almost flush with the surrounding plate, and uninterested in moving. He would have to make his way down the stairs in almost total darkness.

He moved one step at a time, waiting on each one for his eyes to adjust. The old boards creaked and moaned beneath his feet, robbing him of any element of surprise. After what felt like an eternity, he reached the basement floor. The banister, solid in his tight grip, invited him to turn and go back up—but Marie needed his help, and Nate had to see whether she was here. The single window had been blacked out with thick paint, but he could just discern the faint grey line of a string hanging from a light fixture in the ceiling.

To get to it, he would have to move into the very centre of the room—the most vulnerable position he could put himself in—open to attack from all sides. Darkness cloaked all four corners of this subterranean chamber, and death pressed down from the living-room above him. The killer could be anywhere.

Moving more quickly now, and with determination, he delayed no longer. He dashed to the string, pulled hard— and the light came on.

The basement was unfinished, a cavern the size of the entire ground floor, with concrete below and grey, cinderblock walls at the perimeter. Fluffy insulation, once pink but now white with dust and cobwebs, poked out from between the grid of wooden joists that supported the floor above. Just to Nate's left, a washer and dryer sat tucked in next to the furnace. Some distance to his right, shelves overflowed with storage bins. Behind him, under the stairwell, old sports equipment was piled untidily.

And on the floor, four or five meters in front of Nate, lay a long, black coffin.

Its exterior was fitted with ornate golden handles and latches. In places, there were encrustations of blood-red jewels. And, as Nate approached, he could see his face reflected in the black lacquer, like a shadow version of himself, his features distorted and corrupted by the contours of this ageless, massive sarcophagus.

The breathing mass of a thin, black-skinned rat snake, at least a metre long, lay coiled atop the casket. The creature examined him with hot red eyes, its forked tongue darting in and out of its black mouth.

In the stories Nate loved, it was with confidence, and even ease, that the hero defeated the villain in moments like this; but, faced with the real thing himself, he felt only terror.

He remembered Touchdown's fist connecting with his jaw. He remembered the kicks to his ribs. He remembered every drunken punch he'd ever received from Roger. He remembered his father leaving his family, his mother's funeral, and the ill-fitting suit and tie they'd forced him to wear. He remembered a lifetime of pain and—to his surprise—the fear began to recede. *Anger* welled up within him instead.

His scabbed lip snarled back.

He'd had enough of playing the victim, the one who always lost the fight and went home covered with bruises. Every beating he'd ever taken had led to this moment. For once, someone else's blood would be spilt—not his.

An old, wooden hockey stick leaned against the wall in the corner of the basement, amid the other junk. Nate grabbed hold of it and, standing at a distance, used it to push the snake from its perch. Landing on the floor with a slap, the creature slithered into a shadowed corner, hissing and baring its fangs.

Nate then held the hockey stick firmly, at an angle against the floor, and snapped its shaft in two with his foot.

Moving to the coffin, he raised his freshly made stake in the air, ready to bring it down with all his might. With his other hand he opened the golden latches, grabbed hold of the lid, and threw it open.

He brought his stake down hard.

At the last moment—seeing what lay inside—he diverted its course, missing the interior completely.

Valande reclined within the coffin, eyes closed in peaceful slumber. Nate instantly recognized him from the book cover Danny had held up at the Page Turners meeting. The tangible reality of the vampire's existence couldn't be denied. Nate could have smashed the stake down into the monster's heart, if only Valande had been alone—but Marie lay in the coffin, tucked in tightly beside the vampire. Her head rested on his chest, directly over his heart, like that of a newborn child nursing at its mother's breast. Nate could see why Danny had fallen in love with her. Although he'd barely noticed it before, Nate now recognized that, even in her current state of captivity, Marie had a dark, mysterious beauty to her.

Slowly her foggy eyes opened, and she gazed up at Nate.

"Marie, my name is Nate Bourdain," he whispered. "I'm a friend of Danny. I'm here to rescue you."

Her blouse, half unbuttoned and torn, had been stained red with blood, and her face had taken on the pallor of milk turned sour. She'd been bitten many times: on the neck, the arms, and the face. Her eyes appeared to only half register his presence. Her shoulders rose up slightly as her lungs filled with air. Her mouth opened and she let out a horrific, piercing scream, whose startling ferocity pushed Nate back away from the coffin.

Valande awoke.

The vampire moved with such speed that Nate barely saw it happen. Still recovering from the shock of Marie's scream, Nate suddenly found Valande towering over him. The villain's normally alabaster face was stained from the blood of his last meal, partly dried, brown, and flaking, the rest still a sticky crimson.

"How dare you interrupt my slumber?"

A hand shot forward, and grabbed hold of Nate's neck. Sharp nails pierced skin; his feet left the floor. The makeshift stake slipped from Nate's grasp, bounced on the concrete, and skidded toward the stairway, far from reach. He gasped for breath and clawed at the vampire's hand, but the monster held tight.

"You pathetic worm," said Valande, tightening his grip.

"For a thousand years I have roamed the earth. Rivers of blood have flowed down my throat. I have sucked the eyes from the sockets of the world's greatest warriors, and used their skulls as bowls for decades. I have eaten babies and made widows of their mothers. Now you—a mere child—think that you might break in upon my sleep without reprisal?"

Nate couldn't breathe. His vision was a blur of blacks and reds. He kicked his dangling legs frantically, but his feet found nothing.

"You have no understanding of how insignificant you are," said Valande.

With a brutal heave, the vampire threw his victim across the room, into the shelves. They and their contents came crashing down around Nate, bruising and burying him.

He couldn't move, couldn't breathe, couldn't even think. It all had happened too fast. He'd not had time to plan, and now the only certainty was his own death.

Valande crossed the basement with frightening speed, reached down through the pile of plastic bins and their spilled contents, grabbed hold of Nate's hair, and yanked him up out of the mess.

Nate cried out as a handful of hair tore bloodily from his scalp.

The vampire's tongue slipped out from between his lips, and licked clean the blood from hairs, before he dropped them away. "Your kind can never understand," said Valande. "You cannot kill me. I am he who will live on long after you are gone. When this building has crumbled, and these stones have turned to sand, everything you have ever known or cared for will be forgotten—but I will still be here, as always, to steal away wives, to break men's hearts, and to kill and kill and kill again. I cannot be defeated, for I am eternal."

With nothing left to lose and his death assured, Nate found himself laughing.

"Eternal?" he said between chuckles. "You're a character from a cheesy series of horror novels. You aren't even real. You're just a piece of cheap pulp fiction, a quick read while I'm waiting for the bus. You're what people leave behind at the cottage when they come back home to live their real lives. You are nothing but dust on a shelf!"

"Dust on a shelf?" said Valande, confusion moving across his face.

The vampire had been distracted by Nate's words for only a brief moment, but it was long enough. The broken hockey stick penetrated Valande's back, digging deep into the flesh, between bones.

The wounded monster let out a terrifying cry of rage and pain. The stake had missed his heart, but the agony of the injury had hold of him. As Valande dropped to his knees, Nate saw Spenser beyond him.

Spenser had found the strength to come back inside, and in doing so he'd saved Nate's life. "Run!" he shouted.

Nate darted past the wounded monster. He and Spenser reached the stairs, but Nate paused. "Wait! We've got to get Marie!"

Marie had climbed out of the coffin, and was trying to yank the embedded stake from Valande's back. Her nearly translucent skin and delicate frame gave her the appearance of a walking skeleton.

"No, we have to leave her!" Spenser pulled at Nate, urging him up the steps.

Valande remained defiant. "You'll die for this!"

The boys reached the top of the stairs, ran through the house, and emerged into the safety of the sunlight. A perfectly cloudless afternoon sky greeted them. The sun felt hot against their sweaty bodies and impossibly bright to their eyes. They were shielded from harm by its protective rays; but Marie was still down in the basement, under the thrall of the vampire.

On the far side of the street, an old man with a silver cap and a long, grey beard watched them closely.

TEN

LOST BATTLES

At the Morton Weisinger Archery Training Centre, life and death were measured not by spilt blood and pounds of flesh, but by arrows fired and bull's-eyes hit.

Diana raised her bow, aimed, and released the arrow.

Shooting through the air at one hundred metres a second, it connected with the target along its outer rim.

Diana could hardly believe it: she had missed *again*.

Regionals were two days away and, even with her favourite compound bow in hand, her shots were, for the first time in her short career, repeatedly off the mark.

She readied another arrow, aimed too quickly, and fired.

Missed again!

Coach Hester approached her. "Diana, maybe today just isn't your day. Why don't you go get changed?"

Diana had never before been sent to the locker room early. It was an insult saved only for the trainees for whom progress on a given day had become a lost cause, not a potential champion two days before competition.

She shifted her feet, and tightened her grip on the bow.

Diana had gotten used to the pad in her underwear over the last few days, but when she had entered the centre that afternoon it had become gratingly uncomfortable. She could feel it sitting there, soaking up her blood, the same way she'd felt the dozens of eyes on her ever since she'd entered the archery range. With her brother ending up in the hospital, she had almost forgotten about the unfortunate timing of her first period—but apparently it remained fresh in everyone else's mind. She could see the snickers perched at the corners of their lips.

"I'm fine, Coach. I'm just a little off; that's all."

"I understand, but exhausting yourself two days before competition isn't going to help us win."

Coach Hester pressed in closer and continued quietly: "What happened the other day was embarrassing. No doubt about it. That sort of thing would throw anyone's game off. I remember when I got my first period—"

"I said I'm fine!"

The other archers lowered their bows, and all activity in the room stopped. Even the arbalester at the far end of the hall ceased firing.

Diana looked around: knowing winks were shared— they had all been expecting this.

"Go home, Diana," said Coach Hester. "I'll see you at the competition."

"But the competition . . . I need to train."

"Diana, just go. You'll do great. In the meantime, go home and get some rest."

"Fine." She dropped her bow at Coach Hester's feet: it hit the floor with a clang. As Diana stormed out of the training hall, eyes followed her with every step.

In the empty locker room, she was finally free from the persecutory stare of her peers.

If *she* had nearly forgotten about getting her period, why couldn't *they*?

She had been blessed with a natural skill for archery, but with the skill had also come a curse: talent and dedication could make one a target for ridicule just as easily as being a nerd or an outsider, like her brother and his friends.

Angrily, she pulled open her locker door. A tidal wave of tampons and pads tumbled out into her face.

When the deluge ended, she could see scrawled across the

inside of her locker door in red marker the words "DIANA THE BLOODY ARCHER!" Below was a stick-figure girl, bow in hand, blood gushing between her legs.

This time the tears came—they could not be stopped. But they were not tears of anguish: they were bitter tears of stinging, salty anger—and with them came a resolution. Two days from now, she would win the competition. They thought they had her beat, but she would prove them all wrong.

Diana left the centre behind and, after a short walk, arrived at the bus stop. Maplewright's public transit consisted of a single bus, which always arrived so late that any pretence of a schedule had long ago been laid aside. Her wait would be long, but the bus was the only way for her to get to the hospital. Danny wasn't expecting her, but maybe a surprise visit would cheer them both up.

Spenser had no recollection of the last thing he had said to his father. This man, who watched over him his entire life, had disappeared—and Spenser couldn't even remember what their last conversation had been about. If his father had known it would be their final words together before he left the family, he'd not given his son any indication. His departure had sprung on Spenser like a tiger leaping to devour its prey. He could all but feel the smooth teeth digging in and tearing at his flesh.

Until now, Spenser's life had proceeded as expected, in a sort of teleological unravelling of time, one event leading to the next in a logical and conventional manner. Seasons came and went, and Tuesday followed Monday. He bundled up in winter, wore shorts in summer. He always did well at academics, and poorly in sports. Not much ever changed from day to day, or even from year to year. Sure, the bullying had become more threatening and violent since they had started high school; but even that hadn't been wholly unexpected. His life had been predictable in the same way as so many lives were in small towns like Maplewright, where boys still grew up to take jobs at the same workplaces their fathers had given decades to, and where a handful of family farms had somehow avoided being swallowed up by the conglomerates. He had always assumed his life would continue to unfold in more or less this same manner, but his parents' sudden separation and impending divorce suggested that what he so long taken for granted could be irrevocably changed at any moment. When the certainty of a parent's love is called into question, all certainties become suspect—or, worse, turn brutal and threatening.

He tried to remember the good times. He tried to re-call the memory of his parents' holding him and each other in a loving embrace, but when he closed his eyes he saw only the house of death. Blood, violence, and darkness blazed through his mind. The walls of Danny's hospital room, where Spenser sat, were painted a pale green—but, every-where he looked, he saw blood red.

Danny and Nate were silent, just like Spenser. Sadness existed within that hush: colossal and all-encompassing, it pulled at them like gravity, pressing all things down into the earth. Every movement felt to Spenser as if he were under-water, peering out at the world from the depths of an aqua-tic cave. His friends were with him in the hospital room, but he'd never felt so alone in all his life.

Nate stood in the far corner, staring out the window. There was a purple-blue bruise just below his chin, and he'd bandaged the wounds made in his neck by Valande's nails. When he turned and faced his friends, Spenser saw that Nate's eyes, so often filled with rage, were brimming with hope-less regret.

"I'm sorry, Danny. I tried to save her. You've got to know; I tried to save her. But I wasn't strong enough," he said.

Spenser nodded. "There was nothing we could do. She

was under his spell, Danny. After I staked him, she was *helping* him." He was positive that Danny understood better than any of them: Danny read the *Dark Wedding* books, and knew only too well what happened to the women Valande took for his own.

"We've got to go to the police," said Danny. "It's the only chance we have left to save her."

Amazement replaced the regret in Nate's eyes. "Are you kidding me? The police are never gonna believe us. Hell, *we* didn't believe you, and we were the ones that did the spell."

"But there are bodies now. You said there were . . . bodies."

Nate gazed directly at Danny, but Spenser could see Nate's mind was off someplace else. Some part of him remained back at the house, down in the basement.

"If there are bodies, then there's proof," continued Danny. "Once the police see that Marie's parents are dead, they'll do everything they can to save her." His words made sense, in the abstract—but he hadn't been down in the dark with them. He had only the faintest understanding of the skewed reality they were now dealing with. He inhabited an older plane of existence, where that word, "reality," still retained tangible meaning. Danny hadn't yet fully slipped into the realm of ineffable horror that Spenser and Nate now occupied.

All the same, Spenser saw nowhere other than the police for them to turn for aid. "We wouldn't have to say anything about Valande," he suggested. "We could say we saw bodies through the window or something."

Danny agreed. "That's right."

"If we go to the police, they're going to blame us for the death of her parents," said Nate.

"Us?" Spenser was startled.

Danny leaned forward in his hospital bed. "*We* didn't kill Marie's parents."

"Are you sure about that?" said Nate. "We did the spell, didn't we? All three of us." He pointed directly at Spenser, then Danny, and then himself. "We called forth this monster and made him real. If we bring the cops into this, they're going to realize the Elliots are dead because of us. One way or another, we'll get the blame."

"We don't *know* that," said Danny.

"The police are going to figure out whose house you were found in front of when you crashed your bike. My and Spenser's fingerprints are already all over the inside of the place." Nate stepped from the window and moved to the side of Danny's bed, looking like a boy possessed. "Don't you get it? There aren't gonna be any other suspects. Who do you think they're gonna blame for the murders?"

"Certainly not us," argued Danny.

"Who then? A vampire? Give me a freaking break."

"Then what do we do?" asked Spenser, feeling as if the maelstrom that had hold of them was continuing to pull him down deeper into its murky depths. "Tell no one?"

"That's right." Nate nodded emphatically. "The three of us can take care of this ourselves."

"But how?" said Spenser. "Look what happened! We're lucky to be alive."

"We weren't ready," said Nate. "This time we load up with stakes, crosses, garlic, and whatever the hell else we need. Then we go in there, and we stake that bastard right in his black heart."

Spenser couldn't believe what Nate was suggesting: he actually wanted to go back into that house. The thought of returning to that place, that smell, those bodies, facing the vampire again, sent waves of nausea through Spenser's body. It had taken all of his strength to go in after Nate the first time—he didn't think he'd be able to do it again.

"It'll never work," he said. "We were lucky to get out alive. You were nearly killed, Nate. We both were."

Nate shot him a look of disgust; and Spenser lowered his eyes, ashamed of his cowardice, yet unable to overcome it.

"Spenser's right, Nate. Valande is too powerful for us to handle on our own. We're in way over our heads, and we're running out of time. Marie is still down there with him! We need the police to handle this."

"*We* can handle it," insisted Nate, his face red with anger, and his hands gripping the bar on the side of Danny's bed with such determination that it looked as if his knuckle bones would burst through the skin. "*I* can handle it."

"I know you want to help Marie," said Danny, "but you can't. You tried, and you failed. You're the one who broke up The Page Turners. That means you aren't the leader anymore. You don't get to make the decisions for the rest of us. We have to go to the cops. Right, Spenser?"

Danny, his head wrapped in bandages, and Nate, his neck wounds still fresh, stared expectantly at Spenser, and he realized the decision, what they would do next, had fallen to him. He would have to take a side—and the choice could cost lives, or save them. There were a thousand factors that needed to be considered, but his mind was incapable of sorting through any of them. His intellect was of no use—so he turned to his emotions, and the decision became easy. He feared Nate's ferocious wrath, but he feared going back into that house of horrors even more.

"Danny's right. We have to go to the police."

Nate's body deflated like a beach ball emptied of air and left behind to wash up amongst the refuse on the shore.

"They're releasing me tomorrow afternoon," said Danny,

"We'll do it then. The clock is ticking: we're running out of time."

"Fine," said Nate, the fight seeming to have gone out of him. "We'll go to the cops tomorrow."

Spenser smiled in relief, but then Nate continued.

"Before you're released tomorrow, there is something Spenser and I have to do."

"Oh, God . . . what?" asked Spenser, the smile melting from his face.

"We have to find the book of spells."

Lucy Holmwood lowered the novel she had been reading, slid her bookmark between the pages, and rested the paperback on the counter of the nurse's station. At such a juicy part in the story, she wanted to draw out the excitement by forcing herself to take a break.

It was one of those trashy vampire novels, lent by her sister, all fangs and bosoms and tall men with dark, flowing hair and piercing eyes. It wasn't the type of book that would win a Pulitzer anytime soon; that was for sure. But it was a real page-turner, and it helped pass the time during the afternoon shift.

She glanced over the counter and down the hall. The young girl who had arrived five or ten minutes earlier was still standing in front of the closed door of one of the private rooms. Her head was turned to the side, and her ear was practically pressed against the door.

Lucy checked the sign-in sheet: "Diana Fitch." It must be the sister of Daniel Fitch, the teen with the concussion in Room 205.

She looked back up at Diana. There was something odd about the way the child was standing there, as if whatever she had heard through the door had frightened her.

Lucy left the station and made her way down the hall. She had nearly reached the Fitch girl when the child finally noticed her. The look on Diana's face: was it fear, shock, or just embarrassment at being caught eavesdropping? "Is everything alright, Sweetie?"

"Oh, uh, yes," said Diana, though something in her young face told Lucy everything was most certainly not alright.

"Is there something I can help you with?"

"No." Diana shook her head adamantly.

"If you'd like to go in and see your brother—"

"No," repeated Diana. Then, without another word, she turned abruptly and rushed down the hall toward the back stairwell.

Lucy contemplated going after her: the child obviously needed some sort of help. But, as Diana disappeared around a corner, the door to 205 opened. Two teenaged boys emerged, and Lucy stepped back, allowing them to pass.

Both boys were silent. One of them looked nearly as frightened as the girl, while the other simply scowled with an intensity that Lucy found slightly intimidating. They too headed down the hall, only in the opposite direction to that of the girl, moving at a determined pace.

This group of kids was in the midst of some sort of drama, maybe even something a little more serious than the usual teenaged nonsense. She probably should report it to her supervisor or the children's parents; but, then again, a report to her supervisor would mean paperwork, and dealing with the parents of injured children was something she tried to leave to the doctors whenever possible. She decided that the best course of action would be to ignore the whole thing. Whatever it was, it would resolve itself.

Besides, she wanted to get back to that novel. She'd reached the halfway mark, and had a growing suspicion that the vampire was going to kill one of the protagonists before the story was over.

ELEVEN

AS FLIES TO WANTON BOYS

*T*o *suffer alone: that was the worst of it. To call out into the night for help and hear nothing in return, to reach into the dark for a friendly hand but grasp only cold air: that desolate isolation hurt beyond all else.*

On the alien spaceship, there had been others, fellow prisoners, united by circumstance and suffering, with whom I could commune. When precious words could be shared between the abductees, the messages were accepted as holy truth. Brief glances in grey corridors were cherished with unquestioning purity. In the clutches of our abductors, no one questioned sanity or reality. When the aliens had hold of you, there was no questioning of truth: there was only the cold, inescapable reality of the present moment and the constant fear of what might come next. A single question was asked in the depths of space, and it was asked by every human aboard the ship, every hour of every day: When would it end?

But it would never end. Returned home, it was I who was now the alien. Shunned by my peers, as though my madness were contagious, called a fool, labelled a liar, cast out by society, left to walk the lonely streets naked and shamed, with all eyes turned away, save for the eyes of the Men in Black. Hidden behind dark glasses, concealed by titles of authority, couched in smiles of false friendship, their eyes never wavered, never tired, always watched—for the Men in Black never sleep. Their sick collusion, their conspiracy of hate, unravels at all hours, day and night: in sacred halls, bloody boardrooms, and pristine alleyways, plans are drawn, projects implemented, and data monitored, with precise stewardship and unblinking eyes.

I was not chosen by the aliens, nor was I was offered as a sacrifice by the Men in Black: a human life holds no special value to either party. No, my body was but fuel for an ever churning endeavour powered by suffering and spanning the universe, carrying with it the potential to touch the lives of every man, woman, and child on this planet. Earth, this tiny little blue ball of life that we mine with machines, chop down with axes, and spoil with ignited flames, is held in a delicate balance, perched on the edge of a bitter precipice—and only the gentlest nudge is necessary to send it sinking down in the endless void. This I know, and this I tell.

So, of course, they call me mad. When you see the truth and the stars align in the night sky not as a syzygy of celestial bodies but as *scout ships hovering and waiting; when you can't escape the daily evidence of the Men in Black working the cogs of the media, the clockwork of government, the gears of commerce; when you search cereal boxes in the long aisles because you refuse to allow one more child to swallow microchips, tracking chips, control chips: that is when you find yourself alone.*

I was "other" now. The aliens had made me alien. I was without league, friendship, or union, stranded with the irrefutable knowledge of a world others cannot see, and an understanding that evil is not an idea or a word, but a living thing that walks the streets in pressed black suits, serving masters who fly saucers through galaxies so vast and unending that Heaven is but a small room so very far from the place to which they take you that it might as well not exist at all.

Spenser closed *As Flies to Wanton Boys* and placed it back on the bookshelf in his bedroom. Sally Winters's voice, which seemed so frenzied, frightening, and wild upon his first reading of the text, now sounded prophetic. She'd been pulled through a threshold by her alien abductors, and thereby transformed into a seer of truth. Unfortunately, it was a truth no one wanted to hear, and her sad resolution to a life of exclusion seemed a fate that Spenser and his friends now shared, for the unending nights had begun.

Outside his bedroom window, the sun lingered in the distant sky, holding dearly to the final seconds of the day—but it now seemed to Spenser a false sun. It was unable to wash away the horrors he'd witnessed. Though it dangled there on the horizon, a pink sphere clinging to the day, it waned all the same and would soon be gone. Then the night would come rushing in like black ink spilt across the sky, and the world would be Valande's for the taking.

Spenser's heart maintained a rapid pace; he seemed unable to get enough air into his lungs; his stomach bubbled and stirred: yet these symptoms felt hardly adequate. He had stood in a room before dead bodies whose ravaged and broken flesh was now etched upon his soul. He'd battled a work of fiction turned real, and thrust a wooden stake deep into undead flesh. He was watching his family fall to pieces all about him, and yet his body reacted to all of this lunacy as if he had only a slight flu coming on. His flesh and bones should have quivered and shaken before collapsing into a convulsive, withering heap on the floor. He was convinced that his body was just as broken as were those of Marie's dead parents: surely it was impossible to come through this a whole person. Everything he'd ever placed faith in lay shattered and ruined, yet his heavy body carried on about its business with only a minor alteration to its normal routine. He wanted to beat at his chest with his fist, awaken-ing the fatty flesh to the dreadful tale in which he was now entangled; but his body had never followed his commands, and it wouldn't start now.

A sobbing came from down the hall, drawing his atten-tion. His mother was crying. He left his room and went to her.

Mrs. Killick lay on her side on the bed she had shared with his father all of Spenser's life. Her arms were wrapped about her belly as if an ulcer were eating away at the lining of her stomach. She let out soft moans of despair.

"What it is?" asked Spenser, moving to her. "What's happened?"

She looked up at her son through cloudy eyes. "Your father: he was here today." She spoke with an increasing grimace, each word hurting her more than the one before.

"When?" whispered Spenser, barely able to speak.

"This afternoon."

While Spenser had been battling the vampire, his father had been to the house, sneaking in like a burglar, with his son elsewhere.

"What did he want?"

"Nothing. He just picked up some things."

"What things?"

"Some clothes. His toothbrush. A travel kit."

If only Spenser had been home when his father had arrived, he could have spoken with him: he could have made him realize the mistake he was making. But he'd missed his chance. Spenser had been pulled away from his family, drawn off to that house with those dead bodies and into that basement—where even now the monster still dwelt, drinking freely from his prisoner. Spenser had not been home for the moment that really mattered. Instead, he'd been off facing a grotesque fiction that belonged on the written page, but now existed as part of the town, just as real as the forest in the east end, the diner on Main Street, and the farmlands in the west.

"Try to sleep," he said, pulling the covers up over his mother, and wondering how it had come to this.

Tomorrow morning they would go looking for the book of spells and, if Nate was still willing, they would go to the police; but Spenser could already sense that, regardless of what the coming day would bring, it would be impossible ever to return things to how they had been. He doubted that even the book of spells had that power.

Like Sally Winters, returned to Earth but forever changed, Spenser now saw the world in a different light. What had seemed a structured existence with clear demarcations—family, reality, fiction—had revealed itself as nothing but a swirling and incomprehensible mess of chaotic confusion. Safety was an illusion, stability a joke, and sanity only one lens through which existence could be viewed.

He knew now of other lenses—dark, curved surfaces that warped and changed reality like a fairground mirror. And what was he to do with this crushing knowledge? All his life, he'd placed faith in his parents and confidence in his friends; but his loyal devotion to that illusion of domestic structure had led him to ruin. He felt abandoned by hope and lost without leadership. All action seemed futile, for it had not yet occurred to him that he might be his own saviour.

TWELVE

DUMPSTER-DIVING

Nate couldn't get the book of spells out of his mind. The book contained power beyond imagination, and they had thrown it away as if it had been nothing.

"How could I have been so stupid?" he said. "I knew it was real. I could feel its power. I had it in my hands, and I let it go."

It was mid-morning, Thursday, and he and Spenser had just arrived on the grounds of Maplewright High School.

"There was no way of knowing what it could do," said Spenser.

"It was obvious," snapped Nate, still angry that Spenser had sided with Danny about going to the police. "You saw the book. You knew it was real, just like I did. I was certain of it, but I let Danny convince me it was a fake. This is *his* fault. If it hadn't been for him, I'd be holding the book right now, and this would all be over."

Nate could see students through the windows of the classrooms on the ground floor. They were sitting at desks in neat rows, attending class as if it were any other day. They had no idea of the horrors going on around them. People were dying, yet those kids sat there like malleable automatons, blissfully ignorant of what was happening beyond the school's protective walls. Disgusted, Nate turned away from the building.

As they crossed the parking-lot, the school now to their backs, Spenser asked, "How did the book get into the library in the first place? That's what bothers me. It obviously wasn't part of the school's collection."

Nate nodded in agreement. "When I first saw it, it was like someone had put it there just for me to find." He remembered the way the book barely fit onto the shelf. "It was almost as if it were calling to me from across the library."

"It didn't just drop out of the sky into the library, and then call to you from across the room," said Spenser. "Someone had to put it there, which means someone, other than us, is probably also looking for it."

A pair of huge steel dumpsters with heavy metal lids sat together, off to the side of the parking-lot. They were just

far enough from the school windows that students sometimes snuck out of class and hid behind them for a smoke.
Graffiti covered their sides, and rust had eaten away a good
portion of their original paint, leaving behind only the odd
patch of blistered and flaking forest green.

"Which one is it?" asked Nate.

"Danny just said, 'the dumpster.' He didn't say which
one."

"I guess I'll take this one, and you can have that one."

They lifted the heavy lids, climbed up the sides, and
peered down inside. Nate saw a dozen black garbage bags
piled in unsightly pyramids.

"It doesn't look like this week's garbage has been picked
up yet," said Spenser, looking down into his dumpster.

"No kidding." Nate slapped at the flies rising up from
the garbage and swarming about his face. It smelled horren-
dous, but nothing compared to the odours they had endured
the previous day. Nate was about to climb down on top of
the garbage, when Spenser spoke.

"Nate, why did we perform the spell?"

The question caught him off guard. "What do you
mean?"

"The spell in the library: what did we think it was going to do?"

It should have been an easy question to answer. They

had done the spell because . . . . Nate thought back to the library. He remembered many details from that day, but the moments before the incantation were foggy.

"It was supposed to . . . *help* us . . . right?"

"Help us how?"

"I don't know," admitted Nate.

"We didn't discuss it. We aren't magicians. We had no clue what we were doing, or what would happen. You turned to that page, and the spell took hold of us. It was almost as if we were possessed or something."

"What are you saying?"

"I don't know. I mean, what are we even talking about here? Magic? *Real* magic? A fictional character come to life and killing people in the real world? It's all too crazy to believe, and yet we know it is true. It just feels like there is something bigger going on here, and we aren't seeing all the puzzle pieces yet."

Nate knew that Spenser was right: an amorphous threat circled about them, formless but tangibly there. "Who would leave a book of magic in a high-school library, where anyone could find it?" he asked. "Why would someone let go of something that powerful?"

"I think the more important question is who would want us to perform a magic spell that unleashes a killer vampire on the town. Who could possibly gain from the release of a fictional villain into the real world?" Spenser's mind had moved down a train of thought that Nate hadn't even begun to consider, and the mounting number of unanswered questions frightened him.

"If we can find the book," said Nate, "we may get some answers."

Spenser nodded. He wasn't finished contemplating the mysteries surrounding them, but he was willing to go along with Nate's preference to concentrate on the problems at hand. They needed to dispatch the vampire and save Marie: as far as Nate was concerned, everything else was secondary.

They jumped down into the dumpsters.

Nate began digging through the bags of garbage, searching for the book. Some of them had burst, and, when he shifted them about, putrid lunchroom leftovers, three days old, spilled out onto his hands. He continued sorting through the trash, trying not to gag. He made it to the bottom of the giant metal box and searched the corners, hefting the bags of garbage into different piles. Finding solid footing was difficult in the sludge, his hands were covered with filth, and much of his clothing was soaked with grime—but there was no sign of the book.

"It's not over here. It must be in yours, Spenser." He climbed up the side, scanned the parking-lot for teachers—

it already felt like they'd been there too long—then he glanced over at the other dumpster. Spenser's face popped up, with an expression of disgust.

"Just garbage over here too," he said. "Lots of garbage, but no book of spells."

"Since the trash hasn't been collected . . . " Nate began, the realization dawning on him.

"That must mean . . . " said Spenser.

There was only one conclusion Nate could think of: "Someone found the book!"

Before he could say anything else, a student came around from behind the dumpsters, startling them.

"Well, what the hell do we have here?" said Touchdown Thompson, an unlit cigarette hanging from the corner of his smirking mouth.

"We're j-just . . . " stammered Spenser, his eyes growing wide as two of Touchdown's cronies joined the scene.

"Doing a little dumpster-diving, Bourdain? That's how you find your dinner in South Mar, isn't it?"

"Go to hell, Touchdown," said Nate.

"Ooooooh, tough guy," mocked one of Touchdown's buddies.

Touchdown calmly lit his cigarette, never taking his eyes from Nate and Spenser. "Go get two locks," he said to one of his underlings.

"From where?" asked the crony.

"Where do you think?" said Touchdown. "From your book locker and your gym locker."

"But my stuff's in there . . . "

"Do I look like I care? Get going—now!"

Touchdown's friend rushed off across the parking-lot towards the school.

Realizing Touchdown's intent, Nate scrambled to climb out of the dumpster as fast as possible.

"Stay in there!" commanded Touchdown.

He threw his lit cigarette, and it caught Nate just below the eye. He flinched back in pain, lost his grip, and fell down into the dumpster, landing on his back among the bags. Just as he registered the view of the blue sky, the lid slammed shut and darkness swallowed him. Spenser cried out, and the second dumpster lid came crashing down.

"Hey!" shouted Nate.

He pressed at the lid with all his might; but Touchdown had climbed up on top, holding it shut and laughing all the while.

"Let us out!" yelled Nate.

"Please," cried Spenser, from inside the other makeshift dungeon, his voice on the verge of total claustrophobic panic. "Please, let me out!"

"What's your problem?" said Touchdown. "Garbage like

you two should be used to living in a dumpster."

"Let us out!" cried Spenser.

Touchdown's other cohort, atop Spenser's prison, chimed in: "Aren't you used to the smell of manure, farm boy?"

Touchdown laughed.

"Let us out of here now, or else!" bellowed Nate, as loud as he could.

"You know what your problem is, Bourdain?" said Touchdown. "You think people actually care what you have to say. Do you think Jeannine wants to talk to you? She doesn't. Do you think anyone at this school is gonna let you out? They won't. Yell all you want, you piece of garbage: you aren't going anywhere. You're exactly where you belong—with all the other trash!"

Nate could hear Touchdown's lackey returning from the school, followed by the distinct sound of two locks clicking shut—one for each dumpster.

"See you around," said Touchdown, slamming his fist into the lid. The metal rang out like a tolling bell. Touchdown and his friends continued to laugh as they headed back towards the school.

When the ringing in his ears had ceased, Nate could hear the clanging noises of Spenser frantically fighting to get out of the other dumpster.

Nate slammed his shoulder up into the metal lid with

all of his might, but the lock held solid. He tried again, but to no avail. He let out a yell of conquered anguish before dropping down defeated onto the garbage bags. The clanging continued next to him.

"Just give up, Spenser. We're locked in."

"I've got to get out of here," came Spenser's muffled reply. "I've got to get out *now*."

"Someone will come along eventually and let us out."

"Nate, get me out of here now. There's so much garbage, I can't move."

"Just say calm."

"I can't breathe. There isn't enough air. I'm going to suffocate. I can feel it."

"You aren't going to suffocate. The smell is bad, but there's plenty of air. We'll just have to wait until the end of class. Someone will let us out."

"I can't wait! I have to get out now! Help me, please, Nate!" Spenser shouted through tears.

"They locked me in, too. There's nothing I can do," said Nate, powerless to help his friend.

Spenser breathed heavily and, when he spoke again, his voice had taken on a new tenor, one of consummated horror.

"Nate, there are *bodies*. I can feel them in here with the garbage and the bugs and the rotting food."

"Spenser, there are no bodies in there."

"Yes, there are. Oh, my God. There are dead bodies right next to me! I'm touching them. I've got to get out of here."

"Just try to stay calm."

"I'm locked in with dead bodies. Nate, help me! Help me, please! I've got to get out!"

The bugs swarmed at Nate's face, rising up from the garbage all around him.

There is a calm that takes hold of all things when finally one realizes the utter futility of striving for happiness or attempting to control destiny, and Nate felt that numbing serenity coming on now. He could throw his shoulder into the steel lid a thousand times—he could do it until his skin broke open and warm blood dripped down his back, mixing with the sweat and muck—but the lid would never budge. His body went numb, and he sank down into the darkness of himself, like water swirling down a drain. The real prison was not school or the dumpsters: it was his body and his soul. At some point in the past, maybe when his mother had died, maybe when his father had left his family, maybe when his step-father had beaten him for the first time, something essential to who he was had begun to rot, and it smelt far worse than the dumpster.

"Spenser, you're having a panic attack," said Nate.

"It's not a panic attack. It's corpses. They're covered in maggots and flies. There are rotting corpses in here!"

"There are no dead bodies, Spenser."

"I saw them, Nate! I saw them! I saw the dead bodies!"

"I know. I saw them too. But they're back at Marie's house, with the vampire. They aren't in there with you."

"Dead bodies . . . " Spenser sobbed uncontrollably. "Dead bodies . . . oh, God. What have we done, Nate? What have we done?"

Nate didn't answer.

"I just want my dad," cried Spenser.

Nate sat there in the darkness, listening to Spenser sob in the dumpster next to his, with garbage dripping from his hands. School had always felt like prison, but now they actually had him locked in a dumpster. The boxes the world put him into were getting smaller and smaller. Piece by piece, they were taking everything from him. He'd been cheated out of a chance for happiness by his mother's death, his father's departure, and a destiny that allowed no power to come to him. He had nothing to command—not even his own life. The Bourdain name had come with no great inheritance, only shackles and chains, bars and locks. He had begun to wonder just how much degradation one person could endure—when the school bell rang and students could be heard exiting the building.

"Hey! Over here! Help us!" shouted Nate and Spenser.

Soon, they heard the sound of students approaching, drawn by the boys' calls.

"Hello?" said a curious voice.

"Who is that?" asked Nate, recognizing the voice.

"It's Mark."

Mark Neil was a grade-nine student and classmate of Nate and Spenser.

"Mark, it's Nate Bourdain. Please, just get someone to help us. We're locked in here."

"How did you get in there? Who locked you in?"

"It doesn't matter," said Nate. "Just get help."

"Okay," said Mark. "I'm going to get someone now."

It sounded as if Mark had left, but Nate could hear the murmurs and giggles of other students out in the parking-lot, gathering around the dumpsters. Nate remained silent, and there had been no noise from Spenser for a while now. Nate was struck then, while waiting for Mark to return, not by the fragility of life, nor by the precociousness of the human soul, but by the cheap worthlessness of all existence. It was a paper-thin border that separated his breathing body from the dead flesh of the Elliot corpses. The dumpster, the gutter, the trench, and the grave—every prized comic book, just like every mother's son, followed a path through time that led to the same meaningless resting-spot. It would all be forgotten. Every indignity and every joy, just like every moment of agony and second of ecstasy, would fade and wither, become brittle to the touch and sore to the eye. It would all get shoved down into a dumpster without ceremony, and then pushed off the cliff of memory into the black void that swallows all.

"Nate, I'm back," Mark announced. "I've got the janitor."

"These bolt cutters should go through the locks," said an unfamiliar adult voice.

"Good," said Nate. "Cut it all away."

The cutters snapped the metal of the lock apart, and the lid of the dumpster finally opened up above him, cooler air from outside replacing the stuffy humidity of the foul stench and his own exhalations. Nate rose from the garbage into the sunlight. He was reborn from the blackness of the dumpsters into the blackness of the world, for a veil had slipped away and all of life's cruelty and malice stood revealed before him, written on the faces of his peers and on that of this strange man holding the large bolt cutters. They had come to his aid this time; but their masks of innocence had been shed, and they could no longer fool him. Within each of them, Nate saw a sadist patiently waiting for the right opportunity to duplicate Touchdown's actions, or worse.

"You're not the janitor," he said.

"I work at the elementary school, but they called me over for the day. Mister Crawford is sick. I didn't think I'd be cutting kids out of garbage bins. What the hell were you doing in there?"

"It doesn't matter," said Nate, lowering himself down to the pavement. "Just get my friend out."

The group of students gathered around the dumpster laughed as Nate, dripping in grime, exited the bin—but all laugher stopped when the other lid opened up and Spenser emerged. Seeing Spenser, the students recognized what devastation truly looks like when cast upon the human face, and they did not laugh one bit.

THIRTEEN

THE POLICEMAN IN BLACK

Staff Sergeant Doug Alderwood didn't dress like the other officers who worked for the Maplewright Police Department.

The small municipal station sat north of Marster, on the corner of Barber Street and Schooley Avenue, in the west end of town, and it held none of the gritty glamour and drama of the police headquarters on television. There weren't any prostitutes chewing gum while being questioned by cigarette-smoking detectives off to the side of the room. There were no handcuffed madmen shouting obscenities while being dragged to holding cells. A handful of officers and clerks typed quietly at mildly outdated computers—that was all.

A middle-aged man, of average height and build, Alder-wood was neither especially handsome nor especially ugly. He wore a black tie and a black shirt over black pants. His dark hair was neatly combed, and his desk well organized. He'd clearly made every effort to appear nondescript, yet there was something peculiar about the way he looked; it was an odd trait none of the boys were able to specifically identify even while looking right at him, and a few hours after leaving the station not one of them would be able to describe his appearance at all.

Pictures of varying size were tacked across the walls of Alderwood's office, including several maps with lines connecting circled areas of interest. Danny also noted grainy satellite photos of the town and surrounding area. Shot from that high up, Maplewright became just a black smudge drifting amongst a vast rural landscape of forests and farmland.

Alderwood sat behind a worn desk, leaning back in his chair with a look of bemusement on his face and his arms crossed. The forms the boys had been asked to fill out shortly after arriving at the station were stacked in front of him, untouched and unread. Danny, Nate, and Spenser sat across from him. They had just finished their story.

"I've got to break it to you, kids: I'm just not buying it."

"Not buying what?" asked Danny. He'd had a bad feeling ever since they had arrived. Spenser and Nate had met him in front of the station, looking even more haggard than when he had seen them the day before. When he asked what had happened that morning, they ignored his question and entered the station. Now that they were inside, things were quickly going from bad to worse.

"I'm not buying the whole story. A trio of hysterical teens, looking like they just went seven rounds with the neighbourhood bully, come in and tell me they've seen a couple of dead bodies through a living-room window. Call me a fool, but I'm not buying it."

This was hardly the response Danny had been expecting. He wasn't naïve enough to believe alarms would be sounded the moment the police heard their story, but he also hadn't anticipated complete and total disinterest. Alderwood's tone had slid swiftly from casually dismissive to condescendingly mocking.

"It's true," said Spenser, meekly. He looked like a family pet who had been beaten by an abusive owner.

"Listen," said Alderwood, leaning forward and resting his hands on the desk. "I'm new here. I just transferred in from Harbour Mille earlier this week, as a matter of fact. And you see those guys out there?" He motioned towards the window separating them from the men and women typing away in the other room. "They thought it would be real funny to stick the new guy with this case. See, if you go through with this, I'm actually going to have to follow up on it like it's a real tip. I'll have to trudge my way over to Abraham Street, and then all the way back here, only to be stuck filling out paperwork for the next week. I hate paperwork. So why don't we call this whole thing off? You can run on home to your mommies and daddies, and we'll pretend this visit never happened. I won't tell your parents, no one will be the wiser, and it'll save us all a whole lot of trouble."

"Maybe we should talk to Chief Hetfield," said Danny. "My father and he—"

"I don't care who your father knows. You've already wasted my time with this drivel, and you won't be wasting the chief's time—not on my watch."

Danny could feel panic beginning to set in. This is what it felt like, he realized, when the authorities that ruled the adult world—those totems of power in which one placed such faith as a child—revealed themselves to be both human and fallible.

"Marie hasn't been to school for two days. You can check the school records." Danny pointed to the black phone on the desk. He tried to remain calm; but, the more Alderwood gave them that cynical disbelieving look, the more Danny could feel his heart speeding up in his chest. "Call her parents' work and you'll see that they're missing too. Ask the neighbours, their friends, whoever you want. No one will have seen them!"

In his alarm, Danny had risen to his feet.

"Son, you'd better sit your ass back down pronto," said Alderwood, reaching toward his holstered weapon.

Danny brought himself down onto the low chair again.

"Good," said the policeman, returning his hands to the desk. "Now you think just 'cause someone goes missing for a couple of days it means they're dead? I've worked missing persons' cases since you were in diapers, and I can tell you—believe me—people go missing all the time and for all sorts of reasons."

"But there are . . . bodies," said Spenser, even more timidly than before.

Spenser wasn't helping, and Danny wished he would just stop talking altogether. Every time Spenser opened his mouth, their story sounded less convincing than the time before. What had happened to his friends earlier in the day, he wondered. Something terrible, to be sure—but what did that even mean anymore? It was all terrible at this point.

"I know at your age everything feels like it's life or death," said Alderwood; "but, when you get older, you'll start to see the bigger picture, and you'll come to understand that the world is a little more complicated than just the good guys and the bad guys that you read about in your comic books."

"Can't you just drive over to the Elliots' house and take a quick look?" pleaded Danny. "It can't hurt, right?"

"Do you know how many police cruisers this township has?" asked Alderwood.

Danny shook his head.

Alderwood held up his index finger and frowned. "One. And it's being used to help tow Chip Crawford's pickup out of the Highway 9 ditch. One of Stu Donaldson's bovines broke the fence this morning and made it all the way out onto the Nine. Chip barely missed hitting it, and ended up flipped in the ditch. But I suppose I should just call the cruiser back in immediately, given that your ridiculous little tale is much more important than Stu's cow or Chip's truck."

"Let's go," said Nate, grabbing at Danny's sleeve. "I told you they wouldn't believe us."

"That's right," said Alderwood with a cruel chuckle. "No one here believes your crazy stories. You think I don't know your type? I've been in town for less than a week, and I still knew who you were the second you walked through the door."

"Oh, really? Who are we then?" asked Nate.

"You're the geeks," said Alderwood. "Yup, sure as shoe-shine, you three are the nerds, the losers. Just look at you.

You're the kids who have to make up stories and adventures about dead bodies because you're too skinny to make the football team, or you've got too many pimples and too fat an ass to get a date with a real girl."

A desolate hopelessness spread over Danny, sucking the last bit of will from him, and Spenser simply sat there in awed silence—but Nate jumped to feet, his face flush with rage. One glance at Nate, and Danny realized just how bad an idea it had been to go to the police, and what a dangerous road they were now moving down. Alderwood stood, and his hand went back to his holster.

"You can't talk to us like that," said Nate.

"Son, I'm an adult, and I'm an officer of the law. I can talk to you any way I please."

"I'm not your son," growled Nate.

Spenser shot Danny a look that clearly said, *We need to get out of here now!* Danny nodded, agreeing completely.

"No, you're not my son," said Alderwood. "And I'm not your father. But, if I was, I'd wipe that look off your face so fast you wouldn't know what hit you."

"Are you threatening me?" asked Nate.

"Okay, maybe we should just—"

"Shut it," Alderwood said to Danny. The policeman turned back to Nate. "I'm not threatening you. I'm helping you. I could get you boys in a whole heap of trouble be-

cause of this prank, but instead I'm going to be real charit-
able and give you a few words of advice."

He pointed a finger at Nate's face.

"In the grown-up world, heroes don't fly around with
capes on their backs. Heroes are the people smart enough
to know when to keep their mouths shut."

He marched over to the office door.

"I've been real nice to you boys. I've patiently listened
to your story, and we've had our fun. But I'm serious when
I say this, so listen close: you continue with this crap, you
keep telling people these stories, and there will be consequences. Serious consequences."

He pointed a finger at Nate, telling him, "Know when
to keep your mouth shut, boy." He held open the door.
"Now get out."

Nate glared at the policeman, and Alderwood returned
his glare.

Danny saw his chance for them to make an exit, and he
took it. Drawing things out beyond this point could lead
to disaster. Nate was a ticking time-bomb: he could go off
at any second.

"Alright, guys," said Danny, "let's go." He got to his
feet and quickly left the office. Spenser followed closely behind, but Nate didn't budge. "Come on, Nate," said Danny
through the doorway. "Let's get out of here."

"I'm not afraid of him," said Nate. "He can't treat us like this."

"Nate," pleaded Spenser. "Please, let's just go."

After a silent pause, in which it appeared anything might happen, Nate finally followed them out the door, never taking his defiant glare away from the policeman's eyes.

Without another word, Alderwood, remaining in his office, closed the door behind them.

With the teens on their way out of the station, he returned to his chair, sat down, and leaned forward to unlock the bottom desk drawer. It looked completely empty. Alderwood touched his finger to a corner of the drawer, releasing the false bottom, beneath which lay two items: a single black cell phone, and the magic book he'd taken from the old man in the trailer park shortly after arriving in town.

He still didn't know what he was going to do with the book. Its paranormal significance was undeniable—why else would he, a Man in Black, have been drawn to it?—but something about the book also troubled him. He'd seen enough in his line of work to know not to trifle with unidentified magical relics. The universe was a stranger place than most people could guess, and infinitely more dangerous than most would ever know.

Careful not to touch the book, Alderwood retrieved the cell phone and closed the drawer.

He dialled a long number and waited briefly. "It's Alderwood. I may have some new candidates for the program."

He listened for a moment.

"Let me check."

The boys' names and addresses were on the forms on his desk. He shuffled through the papers, and then did a quick search on his computer with the phone still at his ear.

"The fat one, the Killick boy, lives on a farm. Looks like it's about thirty acres of open land. That should be more than enough room for you."

He listened.

"No, no. I just got into town. I'll need some time to get settled. A few weeks from now will be fine. . . . We'll speak again before the extraction date? . . . Yes, agreed."

The call over, he returned the black phone to the drawer and locked it.

Alderwood took a marker from the desk and, drawing a precise curve on one of the maps pinned to the wall, circled Spenser's farm, in blood-red ink.

FOURTEEN

MAPLEWRIGHT

As the boys left the station, the sun had already begun to slide towards the western horizon. They walked over to the rack where Spenser and Danny had left their bikes.

Spenser read his wristwatch. "We're running out of time."

Danny nodded.

"Tonight," said Nate, his nerves still on edge from the confrontation with the cop. "We meet up tonight, and we put together a plan for how to deal with this thing *ourselves*, just as we should have done in the first place."

"We didn't know it would go down like that with the police," said Danny.

"We *should* have known. Come on, Danny: think about

it. When have the adults in this town ever helped us? Our own parents don't care about us, so why would the police?"

"Speak for yourself," said Danny. "My parents love me."

"Well, sorry," spat Nate. "I guess we don't all get to live with a mom and dad who coddle and protect us in a nice, big, warm house up in New Maplewright, with all the other rich folks."

Danny frowned. "Oh, right! I forgot. This is all about poor Nate Bourdain, who has to live in South Mar with his mean step-dad. Listen, man; you know I'm sorry about what happened to your mom. I know things are hard for you, and my heart goes out to you, but—"

"You're bringing my *mother* into this?" Nate felt growing within himself a hatred for Danny, a hatred he'd never felt before.

"No!" said Danny. "That's my point. Nate, you can never see anything beyond your own anger. You need to realize fast that this isn't about your mother, and it isn't about you. It's about saving Marie."

"You think I don't know that?"

"I don't know whether you do or you don't. What were you doing in there just now? Were you trying to save Marie, or were you trying to get arrested? If we were all in a jail cell right now because of you, how would that help Marie?"

"All I was doing was standing up for us. It's all I've ever done. I know you've always been happy to let us get pushed around by bullies, but I'm not gonna just sit there and let—"

"My place!" shouted Spenser. Nate and Danny studied him in surprise. He continued: "We'll meet at my place tonight. In the barn, once everyone's parents are asleep. Okay?"

Nate and Danny glowered at each other and then back at Spenser.

"Fine," said Nate.

Danny grabbed hold of his bike. "Get yourself together, Nate." Still frowning at his friends, he swung his leg over the bent, scraped frame. "I'll see you guys tonight." Away he pedaled, north up Barber Street, towards New Maplewright.

"Are you gonna be alright?" asked Spenser.

Nate sighed forcefully. "I'm fine. You?"

Spenser shrugged. "I'm alright, I guess. I'll see you tonight."

"Yeah. Tonight."

Spenser got on his bike and headed west down Schooley Avenue, towards the farmlands, disappearing into the setting sun.

With the others gone, Nate began walking south. He cut through the cemetery at Saint Joseph's and then, after a couple of blocks, he turned east, making his way down Marster Street with the anger still fresh in him.

He could feel the car behind him, even before he saw or heard it—an imposing presence bearing down on his back, moving too slowly to be just passing by.

"Hey, Bourdain," shouted a voice from the car's open window. "I heard Touchdown kicked your pansy ass!"

Nate turned just in time to see something flying towards him. He tried to dodge it, but the open can of beer struck him in the shoulder and the foamy liquid soaked into his clothes.

"You suck, loser!" Laughter spilled from the window, as the car tore off fast, swerving on and off the dirt shoulder and throwing up clouds of dust.

He didn't see who had been behind the wheel or who had thrown the beer, but it didn't matter. In Maplewright, they were all the same. Maplewright . . . where "small town" means small minds and even smaller dreams. These little country towns, thought Nate: they're incestuous pits with snake-like coils that pull you down into their tiny depths, no matter how hard you struggle to break free. Sure, some people try to get away, but they're eventually pulled back into the mire by the magnet of their own, small-town pasts.

Pulled back to Maplewright, where rumour is the language of choice, and mediocrity in all things is the established norm; the type of place that only ever gets a mention in the city paper when one of the locals accidentally shoots his wife while showing off a new hunting-rifle in front of his buddies.

The city was a forty-minute drive away, but it might as well have been the other side of the universe for a teenager without a car or a driver's license. The city sat there in the distance, a taunting and unreachable beacon of light, where you could walk the streets wearing a mohawk without being beaten to a pulp. A place where plays were performed in actual theatres, with plush seats, rather than in a spare room lined with folding chairs above the local hockey rink. Though Nate dreamed of the city, he was forever stuck in the town, surrounded by ugly homes with bent aluminum porch doors, screens torn and frames held together by duct tape, like those he walked past now. In tiny driveways sat old cars with socket wrenches sticking out of their sides because the door handles had stopped working years ago. While the adults drove their rusting cars and mud-caked pickup trucks, the teens rode dirt bikes in the summer and snowmobiles in the winter, round and round in drunken circles that never took them anywhere except back where they started—just back to Maplewright, where most folks were happy because they were too stupid or too afraid to ask for anything more from life.

This town, thought Nate: maybe they should just let the vampire have it.

But, of course, there was Marie—she could not be forgotten or abandoned. The Page Turners were responsible for her fate. And, though Nate told himself that Maplewright was already as bad as it could ever get, when he thought about the vampire he knew it was not so.

He arrived home to find Roger sitting in his usual spot on the couch in front of the television, the sound turned down. It seemed that he hardly left the living-room anymore.

"I got a call from your school today," said Roger. "I guess you couldn't be bothered to make it to class?" His words were slurred. A dozen empty beer cans were scatted across the coffee table.

"And I guess you didn't make it to work?" said Nate.

Roger raised the remote and changed the channel, not answering.

"I was sick," said Nate.

"Yeah, you and me both," said Roger, staring at the screen.

Something was odd about his voice, and it wasn't just the booze.

Nate entered the living-room. As he came around the

side of the couch, he saw Roger was crying. Nate cringed. It was a disquieting sight, watching a grown man cry like a child.

"She's gone, isn't she?" said Roger, drunkenly.

Nate's mind instantly went to Marie, but of course that was not who Roger meant. "Yeah, she really is."

Roger took a long swig of beer, and then wiped the tears from his cheeks with the can still in his hand. "You sit there waiting to find out it was all a dream. Or some sort of trick they've played on you, you know? 'Cause it's too horrible to be real. So you sit and you wait and wait for that day when there's a knock at the door and you open it and she's standing there . . . but that day never comes."

Roger's eyes had drifted from the television. His gaze locked on to the picture of Nate's mother that sat framed on the bookshelf. She looked beautiful in that photo, but Nate refused to follow his step-father's eyes: he didn't want to see his mother's face—not now. Nate had seen more than enough of death these last few days.

"It's not easy. You know that, kid? It's not easy at all, this life."

"I know." Nate nodded. "It really isn't."

"I never wanted to be a dad. We both know that. I just loved your mom so much that I would have done anything for her. I agreed to take custody of you because it was the right thing to do. I've always just tried to do the right thing, for her."

"We both loved her," said Nate.

"I've tried to do right by you. I never claimed to be a great father, but I tried to do right by you."

"Okay," said Nate.

Roger began to sob.

This is what happens when you fight the darkness, thought Nate. At first it feels as if you might win, but it wears you down and beats you back and grinds away at you until eventually you're nothing but a sobbing wreck.

Unless you embrace the dark.

Unless you make it your home.

"I'm just so alone," said Roger.

"Yeah. There's a lot of that going around."

Nate should have felt pity for this pathetic man who'd loved and lost the same woman he had; but, standing there watching his step-father sob into his hands, the teenager felt absolutely nothing at all. Something inside Nate had been withering away for a long time, since long before The Page Turners had performed the spell in the library. He could feel it in there, getting smaller and smaller, weakening with each passing day.

And he knew now that it had finally died.

FIFTEEN

A GLIMMER IN THE DARKNESS

"I hereby call this meeting of The Page Turners to order," said Nate.

The boys were seated on the dirt floor of the Killicks' barn. It was filled with abandoned bales of straw and odd pieces of farm machinery, its thick wooden posts and beams rising up around and above them. Hammers, screwdrivers, and saws of varying size hung from a peg board above a workbench in the back. Empty stalls for animals lined the walls, and a creaky ladder off to the side led up to a loft. During the day, sunlight slipped in through the chinks in the siding; but now it was night, and they would not be interrupted.

The barn had gone unused ever since Spenser's father had left, and it was long before then that Mrs. Killick had last ventured out here. Spenser's had been gone for less than a week, but already the space felt haunted.

Spenser checked his watch. It was nearly midnight. They were on their own from now on. The incident with Alderwood confirmed what Spenser had suspected all along. Danny's plan of going to the police had been the right thing to do—it would have been crazy not to try—but Nate had also been right in recognizing that the adult world would be of no aid to them. Sometimes the divide between adult and teen is just too great a chasm to cross. If The Pager Turners were going to destroy the vampire and save Marie, it would have to be of their own doing.

Somehow, Spenser had avoided serious physical harm so far, but the psychological shock of the week's horrific events ate away at him from the inside. Something terrible had taken root within him, and he wondered whether his friends felt the same. The bruise on Nate's neck had turned a new shade of purple. Danny's injuries were still bandaged and fresh. Spenser's friends were wounded, but he could see in their eyes that they were also resolute.

He went ahead and asked the question that Danny and Nate appeared afraid to pose: "What are we going to do?"

At first, only the low-pitched, desolate moan of the wind blowing through the old barn and the creak of aged wood answered.

But, after a time, Danny spoke. "I just don't know. We've called forth a fictional villain into the real world. He's killed my girlfriend's parents and put her under his spell. The book of magic we used to bring him here is gone. The police are openly hostile; and no one believes that any of this is going on."

"I believe you."

The voice came from the other end of the barn, startling them. A long, drawn out creak cried out, as the large wooden doors were pushed open. In from the night walked Danny's little sister.

Her brother rushed to his feet.

"Diana, what the hell are you doing here?"

"I followed you when you snuck out," she admitted, walking towards them. "I told you you're too loud."

Ever since they had performed the spell, the three boys had been slipping deeper and deeper into a realm of evil, a dark place rarely glimpsed during everyday life. It took them in and held them prisoners in a cage nearly as solid as the dumpsters that Nate and Spenser had been trapped in earlier that day. Escape back to the world of light felt increasingly unlikely; but this discordant introduction of a new, yet familiar, face comforted Spenser. Diana appeared to him as a glimmer in the dark, a symbolic reminder that a world not yet infested by evil still existed somewhere. Diana's presence meant there was a chance for hope to prevail.

Nonetheless, Danny was frustrated: "This isn't kids' stuff we're dealing with here. You need to go home now."

"Kids' stuff?" scoffed Diana. "You're only a year and a half older than I am, so don't talk to me about kids' stuff."

"This isn't about age. There are things happening here: dangerous things."

"I know, and I want to help."

Nate got to his feet. "No. You have no idea what we're dealing with."

Spenser also stood, though he was still mesmerised by Diana's angelic appearance.

"Yes, I do. I know exactly what you're dealing with. A killer vampire. I overheard everything at the hospital the other day. All of it."

"And you believe us?" asked Spenser.

"Of course I do. I know my brother wouldn't lie about something like this, and I want to help."

"We do need all the help we can get," Nate admitted.

"What? No!" said Danny, shaking his head. "We're not getting my sister involved in this."

"Come on; I'm already involved," said Diana. "And stop talking like I'm not standing right in front of you! You know I can help.

"But we don't even have a plan!" Danny began to pace

the barn.

"You know my take on it," said Nate. "We load up on weapons, go in there, rush him, and do what needs to be done. Maybe, with all four of us, we could take him out."

Danny shook his head again. "Diana is not going in that house."

"But I can—"

He cut her off: "You are *not* going in there. End of story."

She bit her tongue.

"Besides," continued Danny, "in the *Dark Wedding* books, people always try to stop Valande that way, and it never works. We can't just overpower him with numbers. He's too strong, too smart. There is no point in trying something that's already been proven to fail in the books."

"Then what do you recommend?" asked Nate.

"I don't know, but we have to do something fast. By this time tomorrow night, Marie will be dead."

Nate mumbled.

"What was that?" asked Danny.

"I said we wouldn't be in this mess if you hadn't thrown away the book of spells."

"What?" cried Danny in astonishment. "*You* were the one who tore it up and threw it across the room!"

"I was angry. I didn't know you were going to take it

and put it in the first dumpster you saw."

At the mention of the dumpster, Spenser's stomach dropped and his heartbeat accelerated. The hope that Diana had brought with her into the barn began to fade within him. He took a step backwards, feeling dizzy. Diana reached out and steadied him. Nate and Danny were too busy arguing even to notice.

"I was trying to protect you from getting into trouble," said Danny.

"Nice work then! We're definitely not in any trouble now."

"What did you want me to do with it?" Danny was nearly shouting.

"It was powerful. If we had that kind of power now, we could stop Valande—but you called it a fake and you threw it away."

Danny sighed, and the anger seemed to go out of him.

"You're right, and I was wrong," he said. "The book of spells was real. It was powerful, just like you said. There was magic to it: none of us can deny that—not with what we've seen. But, Nate, it was dark magic: you have to know that. Having the book wouldn't help us now."

"Dark magic? You're just afraid of its power."

"The book was evil."

Spenser had gone into this meeting expecting his friends

to have a perfect plan ready to share and implement. He had always been happy to follow their lead; but Nate's and Danny's argument wasn't taking them anywhere, and they seemed to be at a total loss for useful ideas. In that dimly lit barn with the wind whipping around them and his father a long way off, Spenser took a deep breath and raised his hand. "I think I may have an idea."

Danny and Nate stopped arguing and, along with Diana, watched as Spenser reached into his pocket and pulled out a piece of paper. He unfolded it and held up a photocopied flyer for them to see. Across the top it read, "The Total Eclipse of the Heart Dance." It featured an image of a two teens in silhouette dancing before the backdrop of a partly eclipsed sun. "Experience the eclipse during the day . . . then dance the night away!" read the slogan at the bottom of the page.

"The school dance," said Danny, recognizing the flier. "It's tomorrow."

"Yeah," Spenser nodded.

"So what? How is the dance going to help us?" asked Nate.

"Not the dance," said Spenser. "The eclipse."

Their interest piqued, Danny and Nate appeared willing to let the argument about the book of spells go. They sat back down onto the ground. Danny cleared away some straw next to him, making a spot for Diana to sit. She lowered herself down next to her brother, smiling, but saying nothing. She had become, at least for the night, a part of the group. Diana was a Page Turner like the rest of them.

Spenser went on to outline the plan that had been percolating in the back of his mind ever since he had noticed the flier amongst the other garbage in the dumpster. They listened closely, and soon Danny and Nate had smiles to match Diana's.

"I don't know," said Spenser, finishing up his speech. "What do you guys think?"

"I think it could work," said Danny.

Diana nodded.

Nate said, "It could definitely work."

SIXTEEN

THE ECLIPSE

D anny, Spenser, and Nate stood at the end of the Elliots' driveway, ready for battle. The house frowned back at them. Its dark windows glared down on them like the black-green eyes of a corpse. The roof was a scraped and scabby scalp, and the front door an entranceway to a bleak and cavernous mouth filled with rotting teeth and oozing gums. The house of death whispered tales of blood and pain, daring them to enter its unholy dominion.

"This is *never* going to work," said Nate.

It was Friday afternoon, and the eclipse was already underway. Up in the sky, far above their heads, the moon's disc, so enormous and black that it hardly seemed real, had begun to impinge on the brilliant sun.

"It's too late to turn back," said Danny.

Nate knew Danny's words were true. There could be no retreat—not if they were to save Marie. They'd been up most of the night, preparing stakes with Diana's help, and going over the plan again and again. Only when the morning sun had begun to reveal itself had Nate and the two Fitch siblings mounted their bikes and snuck home.

In the barn, Spenser's plan had sounded like the perfect operation—a simple, direct rescue mission. Nate had been confident it could work. Now, under the disappearing sun, his confidence wavered.

"It'll work," Spenser said quietly to himself. "It'll work."

"It has to work," said Danny, placing a hand around the crucifix dangling at his chest.

The previous night, Danny had explained to them how the *Dark Wedding* books described the cross as little more than a pendant of good will. It could keep a vampire at bay for a short while, but otherwise it would be of little help. The crucifix would be the most meagre of shields, inconsequential once the real battle had begun. If the vampire failed to take the bait and remained in the basement, where Danny would be . . . . Nate pushed the possibility of failure from his mind. Failure meant not only Marie's death, but all of their deaths, a harbinger for the unfettered burgeoning of evil in Maplewright. This house was only the beginning: if they did not draw a line in the sand here and now, the vampire's reign of terror could spread all across the town—and beyond.

Nate took the first step towards the house, and Danny and Spenser followed closely. As they advanced, the last of the sun disappeared and the sky went black. Soon the only light left was the smoky corona, dancing around the edge of the moon like a wreath.

Spenser checked his watch. "We have three minutes."

The others nodded, and then entered the house. Death hung in the air, hid in the shadows, and darted around corners just ahead of them. It lurked on the periphery of their vision, waiting to pounce. At any moment, death could overwhelm them.

They glanced into the living-room for only a moment. The buzz of the flies, a grotesque, tar-like mass of insects clinging to decaying flesh, filled the house. The dirty pearl flesh of wriggling maggots spilled forth from the cavernous wounds that riddled the rotting flesh. Valande had had his way with the bodies, and now the flies and the maggots were claiming them as their own.

Nate tried to forget how quickly he had already crumbled before this inexorable foe in their previous battle. He was better prepared for this round, with improved weapons in his hands and more allies at his side. A furious impulse ablaze in his heart pushed him through the fear.

At the basement door, Nate flicked on his flashlight and directed its white beam down the stairs. Without hesitation, the three teens descended into the basement boldly. No one delayed or second-guessed. Nothing else existed any longer, only Spenser's plan and the ever advancing clock of the eclipse.

At the foot of the stairs, Nate moved through the darkness, his flashlight cutting a path before him and glinting off the coffin's lacquered surface. In the centre of the room, he reached forward and pulled the string that hung from the light fixture. The bulb's glow filled the basement, revealing the coffin just where he had left it, undisturbed, like a black tombstone. The scattered boxes and their spilled contents still lay on the floor before the broken shelves; and Nate allowed himself to recall, but only for a moment, that this was the spot where he had nearly died. The basement had taken on the feeling of a crypt, its walls seeming to yearn for ever more bodies to feed its unending hunger for flesh.

"I don't see the snake," said Spenser, scanning the basement.

"It's here somewhere," said Nate, as he positioned himself at the bottom of the stairs. He pocketed the flashlight, so that he could hold a stake in each hand. Muscles tense, he felt ready to fight.

Danny took his place at the foot of the jewel-encrusted box, a look of astonishment on his face. "The coffin," he said, his voice filled with awe. "This is *exactly* how it was described in the books." He tucked his weapons into his belt. His hands were open and he too felt ready.

Spenser stepped forward, reached out, and touched the black casket. He had drawn the unenviable lot of opening the lid. The smooth wood felt cold against his fingers, drawing the heat from them.

For a moment, they all stood there listening to the soft click-click-click of the furnace in the corner. Spenser gave his friends a warm smile full of hope and fear—then he threw open the lid.

Marie rose up immediately, her screeching banshee wail ripping through the silence of the basement.

Danny's face showed openly his startled shock. Nate had done his best to prepare his friend for the state they would find Marie in, but it clearly had not been enough. For a second it seemed that the plan had already gone awry; but then Danny gave his head a quick shake, which seemed to break the stupor that had frozen him. Now set with focus and determination, he reached for Marie. He grasped in one hand her free upper arm, and slipped the other between her back and the silken lining of the casket, pulling her up and then out of the coffin. He held her cold body close against his warm chest, stifling her screams with the palm of his hand. She twisted and kicked, thrashed her head about, desperate to break free. She was struggling with more strength than they had expected, but Danny held her tight.

Suddenly, with inhuman speed and a blur of movement so rapid that Nate barely saw it happen, Valande's fist shot upward from where he lay reposed within the coffin, and connected with Spenser's face. As if hit by a wrecking-ball, Spenser flew backwards, his face exploding in a misty cloud of sweat and blood. His limp body slammed against a distant wall and slid to the floor—nose, lips, and teeth already a mangled, wet mess. The gold watch on his wrist smashed into the concrete and shattered, as a grisly wound opened up across his left cheek. Blood washed down his face and neck, soaking in to his T-shirt.

Crimson-stained fingers with razor-sharp nails gripped the edges of the casket and Valande arose, moving directly from supine to standing erect, without a hint of bending at the knees or waist. "I can smell your blood," said the vampire, swinging a leg over the edge and stepping forth. He leered in Spenser's direction: "Despite the blubber, you will make a tasty meal indeed."

Valande glanced to his right, and saw Danny holding

Marie tightly in his arms. She writhed about, as if in pain.

"Oh, my," snarled Valande: "the jilted lover. I'll eat you last."

"What about me?" said Nate, still ready at the foot of the stairs.

Valande turned, surprised but fearless. "Ahh . . . the one who called me fiction."

"That's right."

Nate slowly backed his way up the first few steps.

"You," said Valande, running the tip of his tongue across his lips, "are about to find out how real I am."

"Oh, yeah? Show me what you've got," taunted Nate, before turning and running.

He leapt up the stairs, taking them two at a time. He spared not a second to look back and see whether the vampire had taken the bait. He sprinted with thighs aching, calves tight and burning.

At the ground floor, he bounded down the hallway, moving past the pictures of Marie's dead parents, and out the front door.

As he crossed the porch, his speed was too much for his coordination. He fell, crashing down on the wooden planks. The momentum took him forward, rolling to the edge of the porch, down the steps, and onto the walkway. His temples throbbed and sharp pain radiated from his ankle.

He'd sprained it in the fall—and lost his stakes.

He tried to stand, but collapsed down in pain, his injured leg unable to support his weight. Refusing to let the injury stop him, he pulled himself up onto his hands and knees, his foot and calf throbbing all the while, and crawled out onto the driveway. Behind him, Valande stepped from the house and stretched his arms out above his head.

"You fools," said the vampire, peering up at the black sky. "You attack me in darkness? I am one with darkness. I cloak myself in the folds of night!"

Nate turned over onto his back, still inching farther down the pavement, drawing the vampire off the porch and away from the house.

"Look at you," said Valande, steady in his pursuit. "You are pathetic. Surely you know you could never beat me in battle."

Nate stopped moving. Trying to get any farther away was pointless. Valande had only to lunge forward to pin him. There could be no escape now. This is where Nate would make his stand. He gave Valande a defiant smile.

"Maybe we don't need to beat you in a fight. Maybe we just need to slow you down."

He felt the quick breeze of an arrow whiz past his head with extraordinary speed. It reached its mark, and pierced the vampire's kneecap.

The monster's leg instantly gave out, and Valande collapsed to the pavement with a startled cry of both shock and pain.

Diana pulled another arrow from her quiver.

She was on a large limb halfway up a tree across the street, her back against the trunk for steady aiming. Squinting through the darkness, she had a clear view of the Elliots' house.

Elsewhere, the regional archery competition was underway, and the junior class was short one competitor. Diana's absence was the talk of the event. They were calling her a chicken and a loser. Parents said she must have choked under the pressure, while her peers accused her of being a coward, too embarrassed to show her face amongst her competitors. They wrote her off as a waste of talent—a cry-baby who couldn't handle a little good-natured taunting. Not one of them, teen or adult, coach or competitor, knew that it was in that moment, far from their contrived contest, that Diana truly became a champion.

In the thrill of meaningful success, she smiled—and shot another arrow directly into Valande.

In the basement, Danny released Marie. She simply stood where he left her, confused and zombie-like, wavering on her feet, while he rushed to his friend's side.

Spenser's face was a mess of red and, when he spoke, his words came out wet and bubbling.

"Go," he sputtered, pointing to Marie. "Get her out!"

"You're hurt. I've got to help you," insisted Danny.

"No," said Spenser. "You know . . . the plan. Get her out of here. If Valande makes it back in—" His words were interrupted by a soaked cough.

"Easy. Take it easy," said Danny.

Spenser shook his head. "If Valande gets back in here, you and Marie need to be gone!"

Danny surveyed Marie's frail form and troublingly distended belly. She appeared almost feral, like a beast that had been caged and starved.

"What about you?" asked Danny. "What happens to you if Valande comes back down here?"

"Just go!" choked Spenser, thick red saliva spluttering from his mouth.

"Spenser, there's still a snake down here somewhere," said Danny.

Spenser nodded. "Go."

Danny grabbed Marie's hand. She resisted; but he kept firm his grip and led her up the stairs, out of the basement, leaving Spenser to his fate.

He pulled her down the hall as swiftly as he could, following the same path Nate had taken.

Out of the house they came, stepping onto the porch.

Before them, Nate lay on the ground, halfway down the driveway. Valande crawled towards him. Several arrows protruded from the monster's limbs and torso.

"Master!" cried Marie.

She took a step forward, but Danny held his grip firm, preventing her from moving any closer to the vampire.

Valande turned from Nate and gazed back toward the house. "Come to me, my Love," he said. "Give me aid."

"She isn't going anywhere, Valande!" said Danny. "You're finished."

The vampire grimaced as he pulled a bloody arrow from his arm. He held it up before him.

"This? You believe *this* can stop me? Nothing can stop—"

The eclipse had come to an end. Night gave way to day, and the first rays of light shot down through the sky, a spotlight from the heavens, encircling the vampire.

"No!" Valande screamed, trying to shield himself.

In a ferocious panic, he crawled back towards the shade of the porch; but too many of Diana's arrows had embedded themselves in his body, and he moved sluggishly. With each second, the sky was growing brighter. He cried out as the fire spread over his body in a rapidly growing quest for fuel.

The clothing burned fast, his black robes rippling with flame. Soon the fire was eating away at his naked, washed-out skin and the meaty flesh below. Glimpses of ivory-white bone began to appear beneath the oranges and reds of the blaze, and the acrid fetor of burnt meat saturated the air.

His nose fell away, revealing a black, cavernous opening in the monster's face. Out of the cavity poured the creatures of the night: thick-legged spiders, long centipedes, and beetles with shimmering shells swarmed across Valande's seared visage, a writhing, creeping, living mask of arthropods, which quickly was swept by flame.

The vampire's bellows of rage melted into moans of agony. Fingers that had sullied the innocent flesh of a thousand maidens burned thin and then dropped away to nothing, the last remnants of bones disintegrating to dust in Valande's desperate clawing at the concrete of the driveway. He let out a final guttural bellow, called up from the pits of Hell, and then became deathly silent, so that all that lingered was the sound of the crackling flames.

Though the vampire's remains no longer moved of his accord, the sun continued to eat away at him, dissolving bone until nothing was left but a pile of black ash.

Across the street, Diana lowered her bow.

They'd done it. Spenser's plan had worked. The Page Turners had killed Valande the Lover.

Danny led Marie out from the porch and onto the lawn. He looked up into the sky with a thankful smile, relishing the benevolent star's warm rays as they bathed his skin. The balmy caress of the sunlight assured him that they really had survived and that the darkness had been banished. They had won.

Then it happened.

It took only seconds—but, when Danny would relive it later, the next few moments would play out in his mind in unending slow motion.

He felt an instant pain in his hand, a sharp and biting heat. He pulled away involuntarily, and looked behind himself, to his right.

Marie was ablaze, fire consuming her hair and her eyelashes, while cries of pain spilled forth from between the lips that had kissed his on that night that now felt so long ago. The delicate skin of her face swelled, then bubbled and burst, before crackling and shrinking into a charred blackness beneath this new inferno.

As she stumbled away from him and opened her mouth, screaming louder in her burning agony, Marie revealed two canines grown long and sharp. Suddenly her scream was cut off, replaced by a harsh, hacking gag. From the darkness of her throat jutted a forked reptilian tongue, licking at the air in quick, frantic darts. Then her jaw cracked and broke. Blood and burnt black flesh fell from her face as the skin at the corners of her mouth split wide, tearing her face into a monstrous grin. The diamond-shaped head of the black rat snake pushed forth from her mouth, vomited up from within her seizing gut. Upon catching the sunlight, the snake also took flame. The creature writhed, a living rope of fire that dangled from Marie's broken mouth, and then curled back and bit at what remained of her face and eyes, tearing chunks of flesh away in vicious rage. She fell to the ground, grappling with the burning serpent still slithering forth from within her as the flames coursed across her vampire flesh.

The heat twisted her body into wretched shapes, and her extremities began to fall away, cascading down one by one, crumbling into ash. She had become only an immobilized torso topped with a skeletal face, cleaned of flesh. The burnt snake hung from her boney jaws, limp and black like a demonic tongue. The fire continued to eat away at Marie, scourging the blight that had become her body.

When the flames died down, then flickered out, nothing remained of Danny's beloved—only a pile of black dust. First a slight breeze, and then a gust, took hold of her ashes, carrying them up into the sky, over the trees, out of sight. She belonged to the wind now, to the sky and the stars, to rock and stone. She'd been returned to the void that had borne the vampire, the infinite space of the imagination, where souls mingle on the shores of misty rivers of energy, and where ideas are drawn forth like fish from the flowing waters and surging swells of the breathing universe.

The moon's retreat was complete.

The sun, fully revealed, washed white the walls of the house, giving form to all that had been hidden by the eclipse and sequestering the darkness to shrinking puddles of penumbra, gathered below the trees' gently swaying boughs. The heat of the afternoon fell across Danny, Nate, and Diana.

Nate tried to get to his feet, but cried out in pain and collapsed again.

Diana carefully lowered herself out of the tree.

Spenser lay in the basement, bleeding, broken, and alone.

Danny dropped to his knees, and wept in the afternoon sun.

SEVENTEEN

THE FIRE

Diana looked down at the sanitary pad in her hand. Only a few pinhead-sized burgundy drops of dried blood marked its surface. They were barely visible. She placed the pad in the wastebasket and washed her hands.

Looking up into the bathroom mirror, she saw gazing back at her the face of the strong and confident girl she knew herself to be. But there was also something else there now: in the arc of her eyes, the curve of her cheeks, the taper of her jaw, she saw, for the first time, hints of the woman she would one day become—and she smiled.

Switching off the light in the bathroom, she entered her bedroom.

Rich sunlight filled the room. Outside the house, the sun

sat plump and proud in the sky, bright as the day before, as if promising the world that night would never come again.

Her bow, ready for restringing, sat mounted in the press her father had given her for her birthday. The fact that she was, undoubtedly, the only twelve-year-old girl in the township with a bow press in her bedroom did not detract in the least from the pride she felt in owning it.

She went to work on the bow. Focusing on the restringing helped her push from her mind the grisly images of violence and death she'd witnessed the previous afternoon. She examined the new string closely, searching for imperfections in the material. There were none to be found: its surface was smooth, indeed perfect. She fed the string around the wheel on each limb of the bow, aligning it with the wheel's groove. With the new string in place, she carefully removed the old one and discarded it, the same way she had thrown away the pad: each had served its purpose, but was no longer needed. Placing her fingers on the bolts, she tightened the bow, and then removed it from the press.

She raised the weapon before her and plucked the new string. It felt perfect.

Diana had fired thousands of arrows over the last year—but never had she imaged that she would one day be shooting at a living target, in the dark of an eclipse, while balanced in a tree. She had come face to face with a monster, with death itself, and yet her aim had been true. Each of The Pager Turners had played a role and, when her time had come, she had not faltered. The serenity of self that her menstruation had chased away for a time had returned to her stronger than ever, and she felt proud and self-assured.

There was a knock at the bedroom door.

"Come in," said Diana.

Her mother entered.

"Hi, Mom."

"Hi there, Honey." Mrs. Fitch crossed the room and sat down on the bed. "Can we talk?"

"Of course." Diana placed the bow on her desk and sat down beside her mother.

Susan Fitch reached over and gently swept some hair from daughter's face, tucking it behind Diana's ear. "How are you feeling?"

"I feel okay," said Diana, speaking the truth. She'd been shaken to her core by the previous day's events, and yet she awoke that morning in good health and high spirits. "Why do you ask?"

"Your brother is quite sick. He hasn't left his bed all day."

"I think I heard him throwing up in the bathroom last night." Diana knew she would need to lie for her brother often in the coming days of mourning. They had returned home together after the battle, but Danny had barely spoken a word. His cheeks were sunken into his face and his eyes dull with sorrow. The grief had stiffened his body and stolen his strength. He walked slowly, and Diana feared that if he tripped and fell he would shatter to pieces upon the remorseless pavement of New Maplewright.

"I got a call from Coach Hester," said Mrs. Fitch, turning the conversation to the real reason she'd come to see her daughter. "You didn't show up at the competition yesterday. It's because I couldn't go, isn't it? Honey, I promise you, your father and I tried to get off work."

"No, it's not that. I was still gonna go," said Diana, performing her practiced cover story. "I left school right before the eclipse, like I was supposed to. But, on the way there, I realized I just didn't want to compete. So I walked around town thinking, and then I met up with Danny and came home."

"But wasn't this competition important? Wasn't it what you'd been training for all year?"

"There'll be other competitions," said Diana, with a shrug.

Mrs. Fitch's face communicated concern, but also the uncompromising and all-encompassing love of a mother.

"Coach Hester told me that the other girls were pretty hard on you after what happened on Monday with your period."

"They were hard on me, yeah. Horrible, actually," said Diana, nodding her head. "But that isn't why I didn't go. I'm not embarrassed by what happened. Not anymore. My period could have arrived at a better time, but I can't plan every step in my life. I know who I am, and I don't have to prove anything to anyone."

She remembered thinking nothing had changed after her period had started, but now she realized that she'd been wrong. *She* had changed. Blood had flowed from her body, it was true; but that blood had been replaced with something else—a new and unyielding self-confidence. She'd left childhood behind, and made the first painful steps into adolescence. Blood and death were now a part of her life, but they would not crush her: she would overcome.

"You know, you kids are growing up so fast," said Mrs. Fitch, smiling at her daughter.

Diana smiled back.

"So how is it going with your first period?" asked her mother.

"I think it's pretty much over. It sucked big-time, but I survived."

❈   ❈   ❈

Ray Crawford walked home from Maplewright High School, towards the trailer park, with the sky turning purple overhead and night pressing in. A baseball cap sat atop his head, covering the bandage still stuck to the back of his bald skull.

His one sick day had turned into a week and a half, and the wound still hurt; but the headaches had stopped for the most part, and he felt well enough to return to the job. And thank God for it: he was happy to focus on his duties at the school. Too many bad thoughts had been able to enter his mind while he had lain recovering in the trailer. The book, the dream, and the strange attack had seemed all the more bizarre the longer he had had to think about them. Given that the memory of the events preceded a head wound, doubt had crept in, and he'd begun to wonder how much of it had really happened, and how much had been the first signs of senile dementia.

It was a terrifying experience, finding himself questioning his own sanity. He'd felt the loss coming on slowly with the passing of time: the languid dulling of the mind, memories drifting off into a misty sea. It was part of growing old and he'd accepted it fully, but this sudden and total quivering of reality itself was an entirely different matter. Aging was inevitable, but losing one's mind in a swift descent into madness brought on a different kind of fear. What was it that the man in the suit had made him say? "There never was a book"? Well, perhaps that was for the best.

Crawford was determined to put it all behind him. He'd stumbled into something dangerous, and the threat had been to both body and mind. How much of it had been real and how much had been misremembered memories didn't matter a lick. It was all best forgotten. Yet, as he approached his trailer, he noticed a light on inside and the door slightly ajar. He could see the faint silhouette of someone sitting at the table with the curtains drawn. The pain and renunciation of the previous attack were still fresh in his mind, but Ray Crawford wasn't one to go running from a fight. Old as he might be, no one was going to break in to his trailer and get away with it.

He threw open the door and shouted, "Who's in there?"

"Come in, Mister Crawford," said the man seated within. His long, grey-white beard went from his chin all the way down to the tabletop. A silver cap was perched atop his head. He had to be at least fifteen years older than Crawford himself.

"Who are you? What do you want?" asked Crawford, moderately relieved to see that the man in the black suit had not returned and that this new intruder seemed not to pose much of a physical threat.

"My name is Morgan." He gestured to the bench across the table from him. "Please, have a seat."

Crawford, who had worked so hard to push all this weirdness from his mind, found himself sliding in across from the old man, rather than ushering the intruder out the door, as should have been his first instinct.

"You recently came into possession of something that belongs to me," said Morgan.

"Did I?" said Crawford. "Don't see how that could be."

"A book. A book of magic spells."

"Ain't no such thing as magic," said Crawford. Yet, he wasn't sure he believed his own words.

"Mister Crawford. I've seen you at your place of employment. You work hard."

The thought that this old man had watched him work, when Crawford himself had never seen the man before, bothered him. Nonetheless, he was flattered by the praise: compliments had been too hard to come by in Crawford's life, and he found himself liking this man, Morgan.

"Damn straight, I work hard."

"I respect your dedication to your profession," said Morgan. "And I ask that you respect mine."

"What is it you do?"

"I am a magician."

Crawford checked the old man's face for signs of insincerity, but found nothing. As far as he could tell, Morgan believed he was a worker of magic. If someone had told Ray Crawford, even a month earlier, that an old man would break in to his home and claim to be a magician, he would have said that his only possible response would have been to laugh in his face—but he didn't see anything funny about the old man sitting across from him now.

"Fine, then," said Crawford. "You do what you like to make your living. Don't see what any of it has to do with me."

"The book. I need my book."

"Don't know what you're talking about."

"I'm fairly certain you do."

Morgan reached into his pocket and pulled forth a knife. He placed it on the table between them. Crawford had used a knife much like it in his youth, while slaughtering pigs on the farm. He remembered the way the pigs' crimson blood would mix with the water, dilute, and turn pink as it swirled down the drain when he cleaned the blade after the killing. His father had insisted the slaughter be as sanitary as possible. The knife on the table before him, however, was stained burgundy all the way up to the handle. What type of animal had that blood belonged to, wondered Crawford. Something told him it wasn't a pig.

"You come into my home and threaten me? You really think I never seen a bloody knife before, Mister?"

Morgan gave Crawford a strained smile. "I do not wish to bring you any harm, but it is essential that the book be returned to me. Where is it? Where is the book of spells?"

"Couldn't tell you. A man I'd never seen before came and took it a few weeks back. I'd found it in a dumpster outside the school, and only had it for a night."

Morgan leaned forward. "What did this man look like?"

"I can't right remember. Dressed fancy, I think; but, try as I might, I can't recall his face. He knocked me on the head—beat me up and left me bleedin' right in my own home."

Morgan followed Crawford's gaze to the stain on the carpet. He'd been unable to remove it.

"To tell it to you straight, I wish I'd never found that book. You might want to think twice about tryin' to find it yourself. It sure felt good to hold, but it hasn't brought me nothin' but trouble and hurt."

Morgan reached down towards the knife, and Crawford tensed up.

"It's alright," said Morgan, as he spun the knife around, so that its handle was facing Crawford. "What that man did to you was cruel, and when I find him I will make him pay for your injuries. The book was not his to take, and—believe me—he will pay dearly."

"I'd certainly appreciate it if he did."

"It will happen. But first I need you to do something for me. The book has caused . . . problems that need to be addressed. You will help me with this."

Morgan nodded towards the knife. Before Crawford even knew what he was doing, his hand, callused from years of pushing heavy brooms down school hallways, reached out and picked up the blade. Extraordinary warmth emanated from the handle and up his arm, creeping like a living thing across his flesh. Goose bumps sprung up, and his hair stood on end, as the weird heat spread, traversing his chest and rippling out, taking hold of his body like a drug.

The entire world shrank down, and expanded, all at once. For a moment, Crawford saw the world through the oily prism of time and space, and then his body dropped to the floor. The bloody stain in the carpet grew dark and wide, swallowing him up, sucking him down into a realm without borders.

He saw monsters, coming at him out of the darkness: the green-skinned beasts with their sickle blades from his earlier dream, yes, but others too—grey beings with bulbous heads and black eyes, as well as children turned monsters thirsty for human blood. Then the monsters faded back into the dark and there were bodies before him: putrid and gelatinous corpses, bloated with gas, lifeless but for the insects still devouring their flesh. A cold pressure rose up around him like the damp walls of a cave.

He moved deeper into the cavern—and an empty coffin appeared before him, black and unholy. His ears picked up the sound of liquid sloshing about in an old steel gasoline can. The blackness was broken by a spark dancing out from a newly struck match. Then golden flames were crawling skyward all around him, wiggling like the fingers of greedy children.

Crawford awoke in his bed with the moon high over his trailer. The sheets were soaked through, as they had been on so many nights of late. A terror like he had never felt before had hold of him. But it was not the sweat, the nightmare, or the beating heart in his chest that had him so scared.

What frightened Ray Crawford was the smell of gasoline that filled his trailer.

A phone rang in a house just off Route 7, waking Ben Alfredson.

He rubbed his eyes before glancing at the clock on his bedside table. It was 5:30 a.m. His alarm wouldn't go off for another hour. He didn't need to be at the Barber Street Garage to open up until 7:30. A call this early meant the fire station was on the line. He picked up.

"Hello."

"Ben, it's Morris," said the familiar voice on the other end. "We've got a fire."

"Brush or field?" asked Ben, rubbing the sleep from his eyes.

"House."

Ben sat up quickly, trying to shake away the drowsiness from his brain.

"I can be at the station in fifteen minutes," he said, getting out of bed, pulling on clothes with the phone still at his ear.

"No. It looks like this thing has been going for a while. The call came in from the neighbours. No sign of the house's residents. It's bad, Ben. It doesn't look like anyone got out. You'd better meet us there."

Ben jotted down the address and hung up.

He'd been a Maplewright volunteer fireman for five years. Morris and Steve ran the station and were on the township's payroll, but volunteers like Ben were called in from time to time when the paid firemen needed a hand. The truth was that Morris was getting on in years, Steve had a bum knee, and Ben was getting more and more calls.

Even as a volunteer, he'd seen a fair amount of action over the last few years. In a rural community like Maplewright, brush fires were almost inevitable in the fall, particularly when teens got hold of their parents' cigarette lighters, and there were always car crashes of one kind or another. That accident that had killed the Fishers and the Bourdain lady last spring had been especially bad.

But it had been just two weeks since the electrical surge and blackout, and now another call—this one for a house fire. What the hell was going on in Maplewright?

He finished dressing in a frantic flailing of limbs, and rushed downstairs. The "delayed brew" light of the coffee maker on the kitchen counter blinked steadily—it wasn't set to start brewing for another forty-five minutes. He grabbed a warm diet cola from the counter as he rushed through the kitchen, and guzzled it down without slowing his pace.

The sun had not yet risen, and the autumn air felt cool against his skin as he dashed down the driveway to his car. He slipped into the driver's seat, but had difficulty getting the key into the ignition. His hands shook. He closed his eyes and took a deep breath, trying to calm the panic.

He kept hearing Morris's words in his head: "It's bad, Ben."

He told himself to ignore the tremor he'd heard in Morris's voice, which seemed to have foreshadowed his own fear so perfectly. He wouldn't know how bad it was until he got there himself. Sitting frozen in his driveway wasn't going to accomplish anything. A house fire. This was what he was trained to do. This was why he'd signed up to be a fireman, wasn't it?

He opened his eyes. This time the key went in smoothly.

He revved engine, and the tires screeched as he backed out of the driveway at top speed.

Ben steered the aging station wagon through dark streets, zooming past the odd early-morning jogger. Most of the citizens of Maplewright were still asleep, and he was able to speed along the empty roads without difficulty.

He'd been driving these streets all his life. He'd watched the town grow throughout his youth, with new houses seeming to spring up every few weeks, neighbourhoods blossoming like flowers; but, at some point, the construction had stopped, there had been a brief moment of equilibrium, and then everything had begun to shrink back down. At an increasingly rapid pace, families were packing up, shipping out, giving up—draining the lifeblood from the town. He'd lost track of the number of farms that had gone under in the last couple of years, and, for the life of him, couldn't remember

the last time a new house had been built. The existing infra-
structure was disintegrating steadily, and even some parts of
New Maplewright had taken on a weather-worn appearance.
Heck, he himself had moved away to a place up on Route 7,
out of the town proper. Ben Alfredson's town was falling
apart around him, and, from the tone of Morris's voice when
he called, it sounded like Maplewright might have lost one
more family.

He skidded the vehicle around a corner, tires crunching over the crackled edge of asphalt as it gave way to dirt.
This road was to have been paved, and a billboard had once
shown an architect's rendering of comfortable middle-class
homes lining the way from here to the next suburban bend.
But that dream had died, and Ben's wheels kicked up a cloud
of dust as he sped onward.

As he neared the address Morris had given him, he
thought he saw the sun beginning to rise above the roofs of
the houses ahead of him; but he quickly realized that that
made no sense—he was headed north. As Ben turned left
onto Abraham Street, the source of the misleading light on
the horizon became apparent.

The fire truck was parked at the side of the road a few
houses down. Several families were gathered in groups, out
on their lawns in pyjamas and housecoats. Morris and Steve
were in full gear, still getting the hose attached to a nearby

hydrant.

Ben pulled over and got out of the car.

Even from a distance, he could feel the heat.

"My God," he said.

The house at 48 Abraham Street was an inferno.

EIGHTEEN

A HOLLOW VICTORY

*H*is bride stood before him, but her eyes were no longer her own. Those windows to the soul, as the poets rightly call them, had taken on the countenance of the vile beast.

Her frock had been removed, and she stood before him unashamed, in only petticoat, corset, and chemise.

The wound in her neck bled freely, the rivulets disappearing into her bosom.

"You have made me a cuckold," he said.

"You have made yourself one," replied the bride.

Such boldness never had she demonstrated during their courtship. He felt ashamed to find that now, in this state, she awoke in him stirrings he'd not previously felt.

"Shall I leave then?" he questioned. "Simply forfeit my mar-

riage to this monster? Will he claim in addition your dowry?"

"It matters not to me. Should you choose to stay, it could prove amusing, if my master were to make you his plaything."

The flames flickering atop the sconce grew dimmer, and the shadows swallowed more of the room.

"And what shall I tell our friends when the cards begin to arrive and we are called upon?"

"Tell them I am become an abbess and I hold candle to the devil," she said with a haunting laugh.

"I could have a constable here in minutes," he threatened.

"I could have you slain in seconds," she replied.

There was something vulpine about her smile, and he found himself growing ever more afraid.

"Seconds? You mean . . . "

"Yes," came a voice from behind him.

Sir Alexander turned and saw with horror that the door to the study had opened, and that the demon Valande had silently entered the room. It was as though the reaper himself had joined them.

"Thou thoughtest me dead, perhaps?" said the vampire. "Thou shouldst have known better."

Sir Alexander reached into the pocket of his topcoat, grasping the rosary beads that lay hidden within. He shut his eyes and began to pray.

"Novenas will help thee not, good sir," said Valande. "For what good are nine days of prayer when I have already been ravish-

ing thy wife for four?"

Sir Alexander opened his eyes and, in his shock, released the ros-
ary. The beads fell to the floor.

"Four? Four days?" he said, the words coming out as a whis-
per. "Can it be true?"

The vampire placed an icy hand on his shoulder. "Worry not,
Sir Alexander. I will finish thee far quicker than that."

Nate peered up from the book into the murky glow of
the digital projector illuminating a screen at the front of the
classroom. Mr. Patterson spoke, but Nate could barely hear
it. He'd been openly reading *Dark Wedding: The Blood Bride* all
class, not bothering to hide it behind a textbook. If Mr. Patterson, or any teacher for that matter, wanted to challenge
him on it, let him try: bring it on.

Nate had seen Danny in the hallway earlier that day, and
they had spoken briefly. Danny's story of illness, even with
Diana backing him up, had reached the point at which he had
to either go to the doctor or return to school. Only Spenser
remained at home, still recovering from his injuries.

Nate flipped the page of *The Blood Bride*, the third book
in the series. Danny had gladly given the entire collection

to him. Just looking at the books sitting on the shelf must have been torture for Danny, thought Nate, and while reading them he too felt the pang of remorse. Every sentence reminded Nate of his failure; every chapter served as testimony to his shame. Marie's death weighed heavily on his conscience, but he didn't read the books as some sort of exercise in self-flagellation. Rather, the books provided Nate with something for which he was searching desperately: a sense of familiarity, belonging, and truth.

He'd tried to return to regular life as if nothing had happened, but it was impossible. Roger's steady descent into the liquor bottle over the last half year had proven that. Death clung to Nate like a virus, and the real world felt like little more than one gigantic lie. Only when he opened the pages of those books, and returned to the familiar world of darkness and death, did anything feel real and true to him. He and his friends had not re-entered the world of light—not really.

The school bell rang, signalling the end of class and bringing him back from the house of death, into which he often found himself slipping within his thoughts.

At his locker, Nate placed *The Blood Bride* on the shelf above his coat and glanced down the hall towards Jeannine Michaud. He caught the tail end of her conversation with her friend.

" . . . these weird lights. No one can figure it out."

Something fired in Nate's brain. He swiftly closed the locker and went to her.

"What was that?" he asked.

"Oh, hi, Nate," said Jeannine, turning to smile at him.

Her friend recognized Nate and gave Jeannine a look of concern.

"I'll see you later, Jeanne," said the friend, making a quick exit.

"What were you just saying about weird lights?" asked Nate.

"Oh, you haven't heard?" said Jeannine. "They still don't know what caused the blackout a few weeks ago, but apparently a bunch of people who live around here have been saying they woke up and saw strange lights in the sky right above the school that same night. Weird, huh?"

"Strange lights," said Nate, quietly.

"Yeah, that's what they're *saying*, anyway. But you know Maplewright: in a town this boring, even a blackout has to become epic gossip."

"There were strange lights in the sky the night my mother died."

Jeannine drew a short gasp, and Nate felt a hand fall on his shoulder. He was spun around and pushed into the lockers hard.

"How many times do we have to do this, Bourdain?" It was Touchdown.

"He wasn't doing anything," said Jeannine. "Really. He was just asking about the blackout and those lights everyone's talking about. That's all. Let him go: you don't need to do this."

"Shut up, Jeanne," said Touchdown, glancing at her for only a moment. "I'll deal with you later."

He glared back at Nate with a look clearly meant to intimidate and strike fear, but Nate did not feel frightened. In fact, he felt extraordinarily calm. He could see no evil in Touchdown's eyes, only the dull anger and confusion of a high-school bully, nothing more. This boy had no power over him. Touchdown had never experienced real violence or death. He did not belong to the realm of night, a place that Nate now called home.

He clenched his hand into a fist and struck Touchdown in the throat as hard as he could.

Touchdown stumbled back and dropped to his knees. He grabbed at his throat, eyes bulging in shock and panic. His mouth opened wide, closed, and then opened again, unable to take in air. He was quiet, making only a slight choking sound as he tried, unsuccessfully, to draw in oxygen. His face changed colour.

Nate stepped forward and grabbed hold of the hair at

the back of Touchdown's head. With all of his strength, he pushed forward and smashed Touchdown's face into the floor.

Jeanne screamed.

"Go get the nurse," Nate ordered, his hand still full of Touchdown's hair. "Go now!"

She turned and ran.

Nate knelt closer to Touchdown. Blood poured from the bully's nose. He struggled to breathe. Tears spilled from eyes wide with fear.

Nate put his lips next to Touchdown's ear.

"I am going to tell you a story, Anthony, so listen closely. The story begins with you threatening my friends and me one more time. Can you guess how the story ends?" whispered Nate. "No? Well, it ends like this: with me killing you. Now I want you to understand something about this story: It is not fiction. It is the future."

Nate stood back up.

Someone had summoned Mrs. Anderson. She rushed down the hallway towards them. As she drew close, the guidance counsellor winced. "Nate, what have you done?"

Danny sat alone in the library at The Page Turners' old round table, trying to fight the anguish. Beating back the desolation and confusion felt like all he ever did anymore. From the moment he got up until the moment he went to bed, she never left his thoughts.

Marie.

Dead.

Because of him.

He could understand that part of it. Her death was comprehensible, in an awful sort of way. After all, he'd watched it happen. It'd been clear and final, uncompromising death. But the part he couldn't wrap his mind around was that he and his friends had survived it all, that they went on with their lives, still living and breathing as though none of it had happened: Danny ate breakfast with his family in the morning and came home from school in the afternoon; he went to bed each night and woke up safe and unharmed in his bed the next morning. But she was gone. Vanished.

Dead.

It was he who had performed the spell with his friends, and he who had taken on the vampire in battle. Marie had never done anything to deserve any of this—yet she was dead, and he was living, and *it didn't make sense.*

Earlier in the day, he'd grabbed Nate in the hall and made him agree to meet here after school. Nate had barely spoken to Danny since Marie's death, other than to ask to borrow the *Dark Wedding* books. Was Nate avoiding him—or was it the other way around? He wasn't sure. Danny knew only that Marie's death had broken something between the two of them, something that couldn't be mended.

He checked the clock impatiently. He would have headed home already, if he hadn't needed to talk to Nate so urgently.

Finally, the library door swung open.

"Where have you been?" Danny got to his feet. "You're half an hour late."

"We're not gonna be able to meet," said Nate.

"We have to talk," insisted Danny.

"No. I can't. I've been suspended. Maybe expelled. I'm not totally clear on the details, but I'm definitely not supposed to be in here. They gave me ten minutes to get my things from my locker and get off the premises. I just thought you should know."

"Expelled? What happened?"

"I broke Touchdown's nose. And some teeth. Might have collapsed his larynx."

"Collapsed his larynx?"

"His parents might press assault charges. We'll see."

Danny could hardly believe Nate had done something this stupid. Not now, not when they had bigger problems to worry about.

"Nate, we need to talk about the spell."

"Why? It's over. We killed Valande. I don't know how many times I can say I'm sorry about what happened to Marie, but we can't go on talking about her forever."

"We've barely talked about her at all!"

"You have to move on, Danny. We all do."

"Listen: it isn't Marie I want to talk about—it's her *house.*"

"They found the bodies?" said Nate.

"No. There was a fire. Marie's house . . . it's gone."

"What do you mean, 'gone'?"

"It's been burned to the ground. When I left for school this morning, I could see the smoke in the sky. I walked towards it, and when I got there the firemen were still trying to put out the flames. Nate, there is nothing left. Just ashes and rubble and black smoke billowing up into the sky. The bodies, the coffin, everything—it's all gone. You see what this means, don't you?"

Nate nodded.

"The police and the firemen: they're gonna think Marie and her family died in the fire."

"So this really is the end of it, then," said Nate, with a sick laugh. "It's finally over."

"No," said Danny. "It's not. I think someone burned

the house down on purpose."

"Who? Valande?"

"No. He's dead: we saw him die. This is different. Nate, I think someone knows about the spell."

"No one else was in the library that night. I haven't told anyone. Have you?"

Danny shook his head.

"Diana?"

"No," said Danny, defensively. "It wasn't her."

"Spenser?" asked Nate. "You think Spenser told someone what we did?"

"No. I visited him a few times last week: he's too scared to talk about it even with me, let alone someone else. . . . By the way, you might want to take some time out of your busy schedule to visit him—he's in bad shape."

"We all are," said Nate sharply. "Danny, I've got to go. Just get to the point."

"The point is that someone knows what we did, and they're protecting us."

"Protecting us? By burning down Marie's house? What sense does that make?"

"Don't you see? The fire destroyed any evidence of what happened."

"What makes you so sure it was arson? It could have been an accident. Hell, we probably knocked a gas line or something while we were in the basement. Valande was throwing me all over the room the first time I was down there with him."

"It isn't just the house and the fire, Nate. There's this." Danny undid the top button of his shirt and revealed the crucifix pendant. "When I woke up in the hospital, this was around my neck. Someone put it there to protect me."

"A religious nurse. You know, you showed us that the first time we went to visit you."

"No, not anybody at the hospital. It was dark when I fell off that roof: Valande could have come outside and killed me. I was unconscious and totally helpless, but he stayed inside because I was wearing *this*. Someone put it around my neck to protect me." He tucked the crucifix back under his shirt.

"I'm reading the *Dark Wedding* books, Danny. Crucifixes barely do anything: you know that."

"Fine. Forget the crucifix and the fire. Tell me this: where did the driver who brought me to the hospital say he found me?"

"On the side of the road, near your bike. That's why everyone thought it was a bike accident."

"Right. Now think of where Marie's bedroom window was. When I fell off the roof, I wouldn't have landed anywhere near the road or my bike. I would have landed on the lawn near the house."

"You're saying someone pulled you out onto the street where a passing car would see you."

"And put a cross around my neck so that Valande couldn't get close. Now they've burned down the house to hide all evidence of what happened."

Nate couldn't figure out why Danny's theory awoke such strong feelings of dread within him. But then he realized the answer: "If someone else knows about the spell, then that means . . . "

" . . . it isn't over," said Danny.

Some part of Nate had known this already. He'd thought it had been the knowledge of the undiscovered bodies that had been eating away at him over the last couple of days, leaving him feeling nervous and uneasy—but that had not been it, not completely. Something else was out there, something more elusive. He could feel it in the air and in his blood.

"*You* can feel it too, can't you?" said Danny, guessing Nate's thoughts exactly. "I don't know when it started, but it's this *feeling* that's been getting stronger. I can't get it out of my head. Nate, *something* is coming."

Nate's eyes widened.

"What is it? What's wrong?" asked Danny.

"What you just said: 'Something is coming.' It reminded me of something Takim says in *Paradise Fields*. It's partway through the book. The mountains have just fallen, the sky is filled with coloured lightning . . . "

Strange lights in the sky.

Nate gave Danny a grave look.

" . . . and he says, 'The Dark Wizard is coming.'"

The gold watch lay in pieces before Spenser.

It did not tick.

The face was shattered, the band snapped, the crown missing.

It had been his father's watch, and his grandfather's watch before that, but the bloodline was broken. The watch would not be fixed, and his father was gone.

Spenser peered up from the wrecked wristwatch to the mirror on the bedroom wall above his dresser, and barely recognized the swollen face gazing back at him. The gash in his chubby cheek stretched from the corner of his lip, across his face, almost to his temple. A series of sutures traced its way along the edges of the jagged wound, holding his cheek together like an arts-and-crafts projects. His flabby body had always felt alien to him, like some foreign thing his soul had been grafted onto by mistake; but now he'd moved beyond awkward and ugly, into the realm of the hideous. The healing would take long, and his face would carry a scar. The injury would be with him always.

Spenser had imagined doing battle with the forces of evil thousands of times. In the war fields without boundary, inside his mind, he had faced demons, psychos, and monsters of the most menacing variety, but never had the imaginary adventures ended with his own face disfigured. In the stories he had grown up on, those myths that served as the very foundation of his fantasies, vanquishing the villain always left the hero stronger, and victory never brought with it the empty feeling that now had hold of him. Spenser should have been happy. He should have felt like a champion. Instead, he felt like a bigger loser than ever before. They'd been victorious, but the victory had come at too great a cost. Danny's girlfriend had burned up alongside her evil sire. She had been lost to them. It had all been for nothing.

Turning away from the mirror, Spenser crossed his bedroom and gazed through the window at the cornfields that stretched out long and flat behind the house. He'd wondered why his father had delayed the harvest so late into the season this year, but now it was clear: he had never intended to bring it in at all. Twenty-eight acres left to rot, gone to waste.

Spenser had used to love walking between the tall stalks with his father at dusk, when the sky had turned blue-pink overhead and a perfect breeze had blown across his face. As a boy, he'd spent hours playing amongst the towering rows of corn. In those fields, many a battle had been fought and won. He would tie a bathrobe at his neck and run amongst the stalks, pretending he flew over them like a superhero. He'd never felt more powerful than when he'd played in those fields. But now, peering out the window, all he felt was an ominous presence lurking amongst the rows of brown and gold.

The experience with Valande, combined with his father's departure, seemed to have infected Spenser with such fear that even his beloved farm had taken on the attire of a foreboding menace. Even sleeping with the light on, he could not hide from the darkness, for his very home was now a place of horror and disillusion, and the reality of death had been carved across his cheek as a permanent reminder of how close they had come to losing everything.

Though not easily provoked, he was angered by the terrible thought of his own home turned against him. The Page Turners had been victorious. It seemed that happily-ever-after didn't exist in the real world—but that didn't mean they hadn't won. It was *his* plan that they had executed, and it worked almost exactly as he had envisioned. He and his friends had been baptized in bitter waters; but they had survived and the villain had been conquered, just as in the stories he loved. For once, Spenser had taken the lead, Danny and Nate had followed, and they'd been triumphant. His father had not been there to aid him, and his body had remained heavy and awkward; yet Spenser had acted with valour and had led his friends to victory as he had always hoped he someday would.

Marie had been lost to them, but not on account of his plan or their efforts. She was already dead when they arrived. By bringing her out of that basement and into the daylight, they hadn't killed her: they had only set her free. They'd given her soul peace by liberating it from the damnation to which the vampire had sentenced it when he had turned her into a demon of the night.

Spenser realized then, for the first time, that they had not failed at all. They had saved Marie's soul, and avenged her death by dispatching her murderer. The Page Turners had done what the characters of countless novels had been unable to do: they had killed Valande.

Spenser reached up and touched his cheek. It stung fiercely, but the pain didn't bother him as much as it had before. He was confident that it would eventually heal and that he would be whole again. In the meantime, the wound would continue to sting and ache—but what of it? Life was painful, and all one could do was continue to trudge on through the hurt until things changed. Nothing was static. Spenser wouldn't be chubby and awkward forever. Someday he would be strong. Someday he would be a man.

He turned his back on the ominous fields, and reminded himself that he was a hero, that they all were, and that it was time to start acting like it. He would reclaim his home and his life. The time for fear was over.

Spenser lay down on his bed and smiled for the first time in a very long time.

Outside, in the fields behind the farmhouse, thin bodies pressed between the rows of corn, swishing amongst the stalks like living shadows under the setting sun—for, when Spenser had stared out his window, something out in the fields had been staring back at him, with black and hateful eyes. Spenser, Danny, Diana, and Nate would soon come to learn a regrettable and inescapable truth: the age of fear had only just begun.

END OF BOOK ONE

ACKNOWLEDGEMENTS

*M*any persons deserve thanks for the success of **The Page Turners**.

My wife, SARAH JOHNS, *and my daughters,* JILLIAN *and* ALYSSA JOHNS. *With every breath I breathe, I wish for nothing but happiness and joy for the three of you.*

CHRISTIAAN ANDERSON, AARON CAMPBELL, *and* DARCY HOULAHAN, *for two decades of friendship and support, and for getting me through so many tedious workdays.*

JOE LIPSETT, *who let me cry on his couch when my world was falling apart, and the only person I've ever met whose passion for cinema surpasses my own.*

BRENDAN BLOM, AN NGUYEN, APRIL YORKE, *and all of the* **(Cult)ure Magazine** *writers, editors, and artists.*

All of my teammates on SCARED HITLESS, STAN'S DINER, *and* THE UTILITY BUCKETS, *particularly for sticking with a goalie who gets suspended for fighting at least once every season.*

ACKNOWLEDGEMENTS

D. W. RICHARDS, *who not only let me copy-edit his novel while I was still a grad student, but also actually paid me to do it.*

AGNES CADIEUX, *who took the time to read through an early draft of the entire trilogy and provided thoughtful advice, while simultaneously crafting her own novel.*

JEANNINE CHURCHILL, LIISA JOHNS, TIINA JOHNS, ASHLEY OMAN, *and all of the early readers, who gave such positive feedback and support.*

VERONICA FRAGA DINIS, *who assisted in both the editing and layout process by providing comments on the story overall, suggesting new wording, catching typographical and other errors, offering constructive criticism of the layout, and even weeding out problems in end-of-line hyphenation.*

BRIAN JOHNSON and SUZY WALDMAN, *whose passion for literature and willingness to lend their home for a three-day novel-writing marathon started this entire crazy endeavour so many years ago.*

JENNIFER FARWELL, *for being the first of my friends to write and publish a novel, thereby allowing me to follow in her footsteps.*

DAVID MACK, *whose character Maya "Echo" Lopez absolutely refused to stay on the page. Maya's spirit quest sent me on a quest of my own—one that resulted in the creation of* **The Page Turners**.

BRAM STOKER, STEPHEN KING, JOSS WHEDON, GARTH ENNIS, *and all giants of vampire fiction, upon whose shoulders I stand.*

My photographer, MELANIE SHIELDS, *who allowed me*

to get as close as I will ever come to living out my fantasy of being a **Men's Health** cover model. Please, learn more about her at melanieshieldsphotography.com.

My cover designer, KIT FOSTER, who looked at a scan of an ugly sketch I had drawn on a crumpled piece of paper, and turned it into the beautiful cover that graces the book in your hands. Kit's work is showcased at kitfosterdesign.com.

DAVID CHURCHILL, ALAN JOHNS, BETH JOHNS, DAVE LEFEVRE, KALLI LEFEVRE, and VICTORIA MICHAUD—parenting (me) ain't easy.

And finally my editor, FORREST ADAM SUMNER, whose revisions, comments, and questions helped improve the book immensely on so many levels. I especially appreciate his insistence on perfection and eye for detail, from spotting split infinitives to knowing what material high-school flooring is made of. He noticed when I was being lazy in my prose and called me on it, and helped to smooth out the flow of my syntax from start to finish. He came on board as a copy-editor, but finished the project as my partner on so many aspects of the book. He created beautiful interior layouts for both the paperback and the e-book, drafted the maps of Maplewright that grace the opening pages, and put the finishing touches on the book's cover. Buckle up, Mister Sumner: there's no time for a breather—it's on to Book II for both of us! (You can learn more about him at brillianteditions.com.)

A Note from the Author

Dear Reader,

I grew up, the child of divorced parents, in a small Ontario town.

As an angry teenage punk-rocker, I felt completely disconnected from the rural environment in which I lived.

I was, however, able to find solace from the difficulties of my life within the pages of horror, sci-fi, and fantasy.

Now, as an adult, I've crafted The *Page Turners* Trilogy in hopes of contributing to the world the types of passionate and emotionally resonant stories that brought me such joy and comfort during my often challenging adolescent years.

I sincerely hope that you enjoyed *The Page Turners: Blood*, especially if you are a teenager struggling with family breakdown, bullying, or any one of the myriad of other challenges the world throws at young people today. As Spenser has learned at the end of Book I, there are no happily-ever-afters; but, I promise you, life does get better if you persevere. So hang in there, my friends—I'm right there with you.

I would love to hear from you, and there are a number of ways you can contact me:

- visit *www.thepageturnerstrilogy.com* and
  subscribe to *The Page Turners Newsletter*
- find me at *Facebook.com/thepageturnerstrilogy*
- follow me on Twitter *@Kevin_T_Johns*
- email me at *kevintjohns@gmail.com*.

I look forward to hearing from you.

Thanks for reading, and be sure to look for Books II and III of The *Page Turners* Trilogy!

KEVIN T. JOHNS
Ottawa, Ontario, Canada,
October, 2013.

The text of this book is composed in BEMBO BOOK MONOTYPE STANDARD, a twentieth-century revival of a typeface first cut by FRANCESCO GRIFFO about 1495. BEMBO was designed under the direction of STANLEY MORISON for the MONOTYPE CORPORATION in 1929.

The ornaments denoting section breaks are from the typeface ADOBE CASLON PRO, designed in 1990 by CAROL TWOMBLY. CASLON was first created by WILLIAM CASLON I in 1722.

In the maps, the centre of the compass rose and the arrows are set in WINGDINGS and WINGDINGS 3, respectively. Both typefaces were developed for TYPE SOLUTIONS, INC., in 1990 by BRETT HAMMIT, who combined glyphs from LUCIDA ICONS, ARROWS, AND STARS, which were licensed from CHARLES BIGELOW and KRIS HOLMES.

The cover and title pages are set in UGLYQUA, designed in 2004 by MANFRED KLEIN.

The typeface in the CAT & BEAN PUBLISHING logo is LEAGUE GOTHIC, a twenty-first-century revival of ALTERNATE GOTHIC #1, which was designed by MORRIS FULLER BENTON for the AMERICAN TYPE FOUNDERS COMPANY in 1903; LEAGUE GOTHIC was developed by THE LEAGUE OF MOVABLE TYPE, with contributions from MICAH RICH, TYLER FINCK, and DANNCI.

The cover was designed by KIT FOSTER, KEVIN T. JOHNS, and FORREST ADAM SUMNER.

MELANIE SHIELDS photographed the author.

The maps of Maplewright were drawn by FORREST ADAM SUMNER, from a design by him and the author.

www.ingramcontent.com/pod-product-compliance
Lightning Source LLC
Chambersburg PA
CBHW021644260626
47154CB00017BA/2246